MURDER IN SEATTLE

A Northwest Cozy Mystery - Book 3

BY

DIANNE HARMAN

Published by: Dianne Harman
www.dianneharman.com

Interior, cover design and website by
Vivek Rajan

ISBN: 978-1974056965

CONTENTS

ACKNOWLEDGMENTS

To Mike and Noelle Harman: For always graciously hosting me on my trips to Seattle, sharing your knowledge of the Northwest, and giving me great ideas for my books!

To you, my readers: I so value your input and your continued support. When I get an email from you asking when my next book will be published, because you're ready for one, believe me, it makes my day!

To Vivek: Who's always there to design great book covers for me and handle all the technical aspects of publishing a book. I so appreciate what you do!

And last, but certainly not least, To Tom: Who's been there from the start. Thanks for always encouraging me, suggesting ways to make my books better, and taking care of just about everything around the house. Who would have thought role reversals were possible at this stage of life?

Win FREE Paperbacks every week!

Go to www.dianneharman.com/freepaperback.html and get your FREE copies of Dianne's books and favorite recipes immediately by signing up for her newsletter.

Once you've signed up for her newsletter you're eligible to win three paperbacks. One lucky winner is picked every week. Hurry before the offer ends!

PROLOGUE

Vincent 'Vinny' Santora pulled down each of the cuffs of his dress shirt with a short, sharp, tug. His long, fine fingers fixed the chunky gold cufflinks in place with a dexterity that came from years of practice. The heavy cufflinks had belonged to his father and his grandfather before him. Since Vinny had no children of his own, one day the cufflinks would belong to Clark Blackstock, his nephew, the son of Vinny's beloved older sister, Valentina. Straightening his tux, a deep gravelly voice reached him through the open door of his walk-in closet.

"You okay in there, Boss? I can hear you sniffin'. No cryin' til' the church, ya' hear me, ya' big softie?"

"Quit pacing, Al," Vinny called to his bodyguard. "It's like an allergy. How are we doing for time?" He walked out of his closet and through the spacious bedroom suite to the hallway where Al was waiting.

"You scrub up well, Al." Vinny smiled. "Nice suit. No one would ever know you come from the Chicago projects, but you could lose the sunglasses. After all, it's the middle of December."

Al De Duco grinned. A beefy man in his early sixties, with slicked-back dyed dark hair and a scar above one eyebrow, his smile revealed more than one gold tooth. "In honor of the occasion, I decided to

1

wear Saville Row, Boss." He surveyed Vinny's tuxedo, dress shirt with studs, bow-tie and cummerbund. "Yer' lookin' pretty sharp yerself', ya' old silver fox. The Cabrini-Green boys done good, huh? C'mon, we ain't got long to get to the church. Clark's meetin' us there. It won't do fer the best man to be late."

"Sure, let's get going." Vinny patted his coat pockets before pausing. "Just one second. I'll be down in a moment."

Vinny turned, and heard Al's heavy footsteps making the stairs creak as he went downstairs. Heading back into the bedroom, Vinny looked around, and his eyes rested on what he was seeking. Walking past the window, he heard the thud of the front door slamming down below. Al never went anywhere quietly.

Vinny paused as he watched Al make his way across the driveway to a sleek black sedan with tinted windows. Al stopped and made a three hundred sixty degree turn, checking the wooded surroundings, talking as he completed his inspection of the area. Vinny knew he was speaking to Charlie, the security guard who watched the wall of CCTV screens situated in the basement of the gated residence, and who communicated through Al's earpiece. Al spoke to Charlie via a microphone the size of a match head located under Al's shirt collar. Al crouched down beside the vehicle and methodically patted the underbelly of the car, the whole way around, carefully feeling for any strange objects, such as explosives, which may have been attached to the car.

Old habits die hard, Vinny thought to himself.

When Vinny retired, there would be no more checking under cars for explosive devices. No more packing a gun everywhere he went. Maybe he'd find himself a nice lady to settle down with. Someone like DeeDee Wilson, the bride-to-be's sister, whom he'd met at dinner with Clark and Roz several nights earlier. Although he was fifty-seven years old, Vinny had never married, and it had been a long time since he'd met anyone he was quite so taken with. He was looking forward to seeing DeeDee again later in the day at the wedding.

Vinny strode across the room and picked up a large white envelope from the top of his walnut writing desk. It contained his wedding gift to Clark and Roz, the deed for a house in the exclusive area of the Queen Anne Hill district in Seattle. Clark's work assignment in Whistler didn't have much longer to run, and when they returned from their honeymoon, Vinny wanted them to have a nice home to start their married lives. The house was large enough for the family he hoped they'd have together.

A long blast from a horn outside the house signaled that Al was getting impatient. Vinny placed the envelope in the pocket of his tuxedo and went outside to where Al was waiting in the sedan with the engine running. When Vinny appeared, Al jumped out to open his car door.

"I can open my own door, Al," Vinny said, exasperated. "I'm not a girl."

"Yeah, Boss," Al said, holding the door anyway.

It was a routine they played out regularly. Although Vinny was Al's boss, the men had grown up together on the tough streets of Chicago. Al was the same age as Vinny's older brother Fonzie, who Vinny had worshipped until the day nineteen-year-old Fonzie was killed trying to break up a gangland fight. The day after his brother died, fifteen-year-old Vinny swore that he would get his family out of the projects and make a better life for all of them. Vinny, accompanied by Al, had gone to visit Fingers Gambino, the richest person he could think of, and who owned a dive bar in the neighborhood.

"I want to work for you," Vinny had said, when Fingers' henchmen had finally granted him an audience. He guessed they realized he wasn't going anywhere, since he'd waited two days outside that crummy bar until Fingers would see him.

Fingers had laughed. "Why do you want to work for me, kid? You should go to school and get yourself a good job."

"That won't make me rich," Vinny had said. "I want to work in a bar and be rich like you."

"I don't work in a bar, son," Fingers had said. "I own the bar."

"Right," Vinny had said, looking the older man straight in the eye. "And I'm not going anywhere until you show me how. Tell me what I need to do."

"Get out of here before you get into trouble, son," Fingers had warned him, but Vinny had stuffed his hands deep into his pockets and stood his ground. He'd just lost his brother, he was scared, and out of options.

Fingers' face had softened. "You hungry?"

Vinny had nodded.

"You look half-starved. Let's get you something to eat, kiddo, and you can tell Uncle Fingers all about it."

Fingers and young Vinny had bonded over a meal of burgers and French fries, washed down with a soda, which Vinny always remembered as one of the most delicious meals of his life. Fingers had taken a liking to Vinny, and given him a job in the evenings and weekends. Vinny started off sweeping the floor, collecting bottles, and washing glasses, since he was too young to be a bartender.

After a while, he quit school and became a runner, delivering messages and packages at Fingers' behest. Vinny never asked what was in the packets, although he suspected it was money. Al went along on the deliveries with him, and never left his side, even when they found themselves in some dangerous circumstances. Vinny and Al were a winning team who proved their loyalty to Fingers, and were rewarded with more money, responsibility, and excitement than either of them had ever dreamed. They lived by a strict code of ethics. The fact that those ethics were on the wrong side of the law didn't concern either of them at such a young age. By the time they were older and wiser, it was too late to get out, even if they'd wanted

4

to.

After forty-some odd years in the Mob, Vinny knew he was lucky to still be around. If it wasn't for Al, he would have been dead long ago. He'd moved to Seattle from Chicago several years earlier to be closer to Clark after Clark's mother, Vinny's sister, had died. Clark's father predeceased his wife, and Clark had no other family.

Vinny would have retired when he left Chicago, but his Mob connections had persuaded him to bring back the topless bars and prostitution business in Seattle that had pretty much ended when the Colonnas had been indicted and forced out of business. He'd agreed on the condition that Al came with him. Now that he'd just about wrapped that business up, he was ready to start thinking about a normal retirement. Preferably one that involved golf, several vacations a year, and a nice woman he could share his life with.

"We should talk about taking some time off," Vinny said from the back seat, as Al snaked the car through the streets of downtown Seattle. The sidewalks were adorned with festive lights. Crowds of pedestrians laden with bags were out in full force, shopping for the holidays. "Hang up our boots. Do you still have that place in the Caribbean?"

"Sure do, Boss," Al said as he turned into the parking lot of the church. "It's my little piece of paradise. You should check it out sometime. I know you like them fancy places like Monaco when you go away, but sometimes it's the simple things in life that count. Sunshine, a bottle of rum, and..."

"Good company?" Vinny finished Al's sentence. Vinny's steely gaze drifted toward the stylish woman in a blush-colored silk shift dress and jacket who was standing outside the church. It was DeeDee Wilson, the same woman he'd admired at dinner three nights earlier. She was talking in an animated fashion with a younger woman in a faux-fur wrap and a long dress in the same blush-colored shade. Judging by the resemblance, he assumed it was her daughter.

Vinny was disappointed that by the time he and Al had gotten out of his car and walked toward the entrance of the beautiful old stone building that was the Seattle First Presbyterian church, the women had moved across the parking lot to the white vintage bridal car which had just pulled up. He heard a lot of squawking and squealing from that direction and raised an eyebrow at Al. *Women and weddings.* He would never understand it.

A hand jerked his elbow and Vinny instinctively reached inside his jacket for his gun. Al did the same. The men turned in unison to meet the owner of the hand, a not unattractive brunette in a navy suit.

"Hello, I'm Francesca Murphy, the wedding planner. Please, follow me, gentleman," she hissed at them. Both men's hands dropped away from their concealed weapons. "The groom is waiting. Let me show you inside. This way, please."

Al, who had removed his sunglasses, rolled an eye at Vinny, who in turn suppressed a laugh. Francesca The Wedding Planner turned and glared at him, and Vinny covered his smile with his hand and started to cough. If things didn't work out for Francesca in the wedding planning business, he thought she'd make a great interrogator for the Mob. Her death stare would be an asset.

"There's something sticking out of your pocket, sir," Francesca said to Vinny. "Be careful you don't drop it."

"Thanks," Vinny said, reaching for the envelope. "I wouldn't want to lose it. It's my wedding present to the happy couple."

"That's nice of you to give them a check," Francesca said.

"Oh, it's not a check," Vinny said. "It's the deed for their new home on Queen Anne Hill."

Francesca's eyes widened. "That's a very generous gift. They certainly are a lucky couple. I doubt if I'll get anything that nice when I get married next Spring. I hope they'll appreciate it."

"Oh, I'm sure they will," Vinny said. "I'd rather give it to Clark now than for him to wait until I'm dead to inherit my estate. Hopefully that will be a long way off in the future, so he might as well enjoy it now."

"Of course," Francesca said, pursing her lips, and continuing the rest of the way down the hallway in silence. The men obediently followed her into a side room where Clark stood waiting along with the other groomsman.

"If you'll excuse me, the bride has arrived," Francesca said in a curt tone. She gave a pointed look at the clock on the wall. It was 3:50 p.m. "See you in ten minutes sharp," she said, before hurrying off with a frown on her face.

"This is my friend John," Clark said. "John, I'd like you to meet my Uncle Vinny, and his main man, Al."

Both men shook John's hand, and Al beamed at Clark. "You don't look nervous at all, Clark. It's great to see you lookin' so happy." Al looked across at John. "How 'bout we give these two a few minutes? See you on the other side, guys."

John followed Al out of the room, and Vinny greeted his nephew with a hug and a slap on the back.

"Al's right," Vinny said, wiping a tear away from his eye. "I wish your mama was here to see you today. I'm very proud and honored to be your best man. It means the world to me, thank you. Here, I want to give you this. A wedding gift for you and Roz from me." He handed the white envelope to Clark.

Clark hesitated. "You don't need to give me anything, Uncle Vinny. I'm just grateful for everything you've done for me already. We both are, Roz and me. And paying for the wedding and the honeymoon is more than enough of a gift. Really."

"Nonsense. You deserve it. Open it later, on your honeymoon. Roz is a great girl. And her sister, DeeDee, has done a lot to help with the wedding. I'd like to thank her properly. Maybe you could give me her telephone number."

Clark grinned at Vinny. "You know she has a boyfriend, Uncle Vinny?"

Vinny smiled. "There's no ring on her finger, son."

Not yet anyway, thought Vinny.

*****

Vinny leaned back in his chair at the reception which was being held at The Catch restaurant in Madison Park on Lake Washington. The venue had been chosen by DeeDee, the bride's sister, and Vinny thought she had impeccable taste. Situated in an area of old mansions and wealth, it was a popular place for wedding receptions. It didn't come cheap, and Vinny was picking up the tab, but it had been worth every penny.

The thirty or so tables seating ten each, which had been decorated beautifully with floral centerpieces of orchids and set with fine silver at the start of the dinner, were now strewn with wine glasses as the party got into full swing. Vinny had instructed the restaurant that there was to be an open bar for the entire evening, although he never drank alcohol himself. He preferred to have the full use of his faculties at all times.

After the speeches, Clark and Roz had led the dancing with their first dance together as a married couple to Van Morrison's 'Brown-Eyed Girl,' and the guests had been dancing to the sounds of the band ever since. Vinny had even taken a spin around the dance floor with Roz and officially welcomed her to the family, before sitting down again.

Now, Vinny was watching DeeDee slow dance with the man that he assumed was her boyfriend. As he recalled, Clark had said his name was Jake. They looked to be having lot of fun together.

"You decidin' whether to cut in?" Al asked him.

Vinny nodded. "Not much gets past you, Al, does it. I was considering it, but it looks like nothing could pull those two apart tonight."

"I'm sure we could think of somethin'," Al said, cracking his chunky knuckles.

"Not tonight, Al." Vinny chuckled, "but you're right, I'll have to think of something. It's getting past my bedtime. Let's leave the younger party animals to it. I just want to speak to Clark, then I'll meet you outside. I won't be much longer."

"Sure thing, Boss," Al said, standing up. "I'll start the car."

Vinny looked around for Clark, who was no longer on the dance floor. The bride was leading a locomotion dance train around the room with her girlfriends.

"Leaving so soon?" said a woman's voice in Vinny's ear.

Vinny turned. He forced a smile. "Theresa, how lovely to see you again."

Theresa Larkin, the wife of his first cousin, Cecil, stood with her arms folded beside his chair.

"Isn't it just," Theresa said. "That was quite some toast you gave earlier. It had me all choked up."

"I'm glad you enjoyed it," Vinny answered. "I meant every word. Clark's a great guy, and he's met a lovely woman to settle down with. I'm sure you're very happy for them too."

"Of course," Theresa said through gritted teeth.

"If you'll excuse me, I think I see the man himself. I want to have a word with him before I leave. Goodnight, Theresa. Do give my regards to Cecil. I hope to see you both soon. Dinner, perhaps? On me, of course."

Vinny stood, straightened his jacket, and nodded at Theresa. He turned and walked across the room towards Clark, who he'd spotted standing at the bar with John.

"Uncle Vinny," Clark beamed. "I hope you're enjoying yourself. Everything is superb, don't you think? It's been a great day from start to finish. I want to thank you again for your part in it."

"No thanks are necessary, Clark. It's been my pleasure." Vinny gave his nephew a warm smile. "You put that envelope I gave you somewhere safe, right?"

"Yes, Jake has all of the envelopes for safekeeping."

"Good," Vinny said. "I'm going to duck out the back way to get away from that awful woman, Theresa Larkin. Al's waiting with the engine running for a quick getaway. Give my love to Roz, and I'll see you both when you get back."

The men shook hands and Clark pressed something into Vinny's palm. Vinny walked through the side doors of the restaurant into the gardens, and peered at the business card in his hand.

DeeDee Wilson. Deelish Catering.

He turned the card over, and there was DeeDee's phone number on the back.

With a smile, Vinny pulled a fat cigar out of his pocket and lit up. Heading in the direction of the lake, he puffed the cigar and blew out a ring of smoke, thinking about Theresa Larkin. Did she really think he hadn't seen her look of anger when he'd said during the toast about how proud he was of Clark? When he'd referred to him as the son he'd never had and told everybody at the reception that Clark was his sole heir? Theresa's face had turned red, and she'd ranted in Cecil's ear throughout the rest of Vinny's speech.

Vinny walked across the wet grass. The expanse of Lake Washington glistened in the moonlight. The snap of a twig caused him to pause. He hadn't stepped on one, so there must be someone else there...

Before he could turn, he felt the cold steel of a pistol being pressed into the back of his skull. The gun pushed him forward, and he kept walking, as slowly as possible, stalling for time. He wasn't sure how long it would take Al to get there, but Al had never let him down yet. He puffed on the cigar, maybe the last one he'd ever have.

As Vinny's life flashed before him, he thought of all the people who might want him dead. There had been many over the years, mostly from the Chicago or Seattle Mafia. Or perhaps even someone he knew better than that? Clark was his sole heir after all, and had a lot to gain from his death. Or maybe...

"Keep walking," said the voice holding the gun, jabbing it into his back and pushing him farther toward the edge of the lake. It took Vinny a moment or two to place the voice, but by then it was too late.

Two shots, muffled by a silencer, and a push into the water, and Vinny Santora was gone.

CHAPTER ONE

Sean Meade walked down the path of his small unkempt garden to the mailbox at the end. The weeds that had grown during the summer months while he'd been away working in Whistler had long since died, leaving brown clumps in between the cracked paving stones. Soggy, rotting leaves lay piled up on the lawn, having never been cleared during the Fall. Sean sighed. He had a short vacation that he was spending at home in Seattle before heading back to the engineering project he was working on in Whistler. The last thing he wanted to do while he was at home was lawn and garden maintenance.

He opened the mailbox, which was stuffed so full that the mail was squashed inside. Lifting out a handful, he noticed most of it appeared to be marketing junk and bills. He saw that he was still receiving his wife Denise's credit card bills, even though she'd left him almost a year before. There was one item near the bottom of the stack, a stiff, cream-colored envelope, that immediately stood out from the rest of the mail. He pulled it out and squinted at his name and address which was written on the front in fountain pen in a fancy script. Turning the envelope over, it had a wax seal on the back and the sender details embossed in gold.

Roz Lawson and Clark Blackstock.

Sean's lip curled in disgust. It was probably a wedding invitation to his clean cut co-worker's wedding to that bubbly girlfriend of his. Ever since Clark Blackstock had been moved onto the same team as Sean for the new high speed ski lift in Whistler, Clark had done nothing but rub Sean's face in the happy perfection that was Clark's life. Despite the envy that rankled him when he saw Clark and Roz together, Sean felt smug in the knowledge that their happiness wouldn't last. Sean had learned that from experience. Five years earlier, before his wedding to Denise, he, too, had thought he was the happiest man in the world, walking on air. The cracks began to show up on their honeymoon, and things went slowly downhill from there. Sean was certain Clark would find out soon enough that marriage wasn't all hearts and roses.

"Daddy, daddy," called a high-pitched voice from inside the house. "I'm scared, daddy. There's a spider in here."

Sean hurried back inside to where his three-year-old daughter, Maddie, stood crying in the hallway. She clutched a doll with matted hair and was trailing a pink blanket behind her. It was that stupid blankie Denise let her take everywhere. No wonder the child had issues.

"Shh, honey, daddy's here," Sean said, dumping the mail on top of the dresser in the entryway and scooping his daughter up in his arms. He held her tight, inhaling her scent. Although Maddie was spending the day with her father, his ex would pick her up later and take her back to Denise's parent's house, where Denise and Maddie were staying until the divorce was finalized.

"Let her stay with me tonight," Sean had pleaded with Denise when she'd dropped Maddie off with him that morning on her way to work. "I'm only home for a few days, and then I have to go back to Whistler."

"That's not my problem. It's not a weekend," Denise had snapped. "And anyway, you miss the weekends you're supposed to have her. Here's her things," she said, shoving a Dora The Explorer backpack into Sean's chest. "No sugary snacks, she needs a nap at 3:00 p.m. sharp, and make sure she's ready to leave at 5:30 p.m.. And don't bother coming out to the car with Maddie, because it only upsets her."

"Right. Good idea," Sean had said. "I could do without the drama myself." His heart seemed to break a little bit more every time he had to say goodbye to his daughter.

"My heart feels for you," Denise had said sarcastically, rolling her eyes before walking away without a backward glance.

While the small marital home he was staying in now remained unsold, Sean had initially harbored faint hopes of a reconciliation with his wife. That was another reason he'd been happy for the place to fall into disrepair, so it would be less appealing to prospective buyers. But the way Denise looked at him these days, like he was some sort of sad failure, he was pretty sure a reconciliation was out of the question.

He settled Maddie on the living room sofa, after making a show of checking for spiders until she was satisfied it was safe. "See?" Sean said, shaking the pillows. "They're all gone."

Maddie stared at him with a look of disapproval. Apparently, she'd learned that expression from her mother.

"I'm hungry," Maddie wailed. "Wanna pizza!"

Sean knew the refrigerator was empty. He'd arrived back from Whistler late the night before without stopping at the grocery store. He could call for take-out, but he suspected that Denise would not approve. Plus it was only 11:00 in the morning, probably too early for lunch even by his standards.

"Okay, honey," Sean said, switching the television channel to the Cartoon Network. "Why don't you watch some shows, and daddy will take you out for lunch soon? What kind of pizza do you like?"

"Peppawoni," Maddie said, sucking her thumb.

"You got it," Sean said, exhaling. He wandered back into the hallway and took the mail from the dresser. Setting the cream-colored envelope aside without opening it, he threw some of the gaudy junk mail items into the trash basket before noticing an envelope from his employer, the Brownsdale-Evans Engineering Company.

Sean's curiosity was piqued. Company mail was unusual, unless it was something important. He knew the company profits were up due to their work on several large projects, including a floating bridge in Washington state as well as the Whistler ski lift he was working on.

Maybe it's a holiday bonus, Sean thought to himself. With his legal expenses mounting, Sean's current financial situation was an endless drain on his checking account. He'd need to be careful Denise didn't learn about any windfall, or she'd be expecting half of it. *What's hers is hers, and what's mine is hers,* Sean was fond of telling anyone who would listen. A bonus would be something to show for all the hard work he'd put in at the company, but so far it seemed to have gone unnoticed. Clark was the golden boy at work, probably something to do with the fact that a rich uncle of his seemed to pull the strings in some way.

The hairs on Sean's neck stood up when he thought of Clark, and his privileged life. Clark had no clue what it was like to still be paying off a student debt fifteen years after graduation, or to lose his family, his home, and his self-respect.

He tore the envelope open and unfolded the letter, scanning its contents in disbelief.

The Brownsdale-Evans Engineering Company is delighted to announce….

"Daddy, daddy," Maddie screeched. "Wanna lolly."

Sean held his breath. His heart was racing. This could not be true.

…The promotion of Clark Blackstock to junior partner, effective January 1st. Clark has been a valued member of the firm since…

There followed a glowing biography of Clark's career. A straight "A" student, he'd graduated from Yale with honors. Additionally, he was a member of the Washington state pro bono and local community affairs team, and on and on. And on. Was there no end to the brilliance of Clark Preppy Boy Dorkstock?

Sean slammed his fist on the dresser. Maddie had wandered into the hallway and observed him with wide, frightened eyes.

"Go and watch television, honey," Sean said, forcing a smile. *Count to ten.* He could hear the calm voice of his anger management counselor in his head. *Deep breaths.* "Daddy will be there in a minute."

Sean raked a hand through his hair. He couldn't understand why Clark had been promoted, and not him. Sean had been with the company longer, and his work was every bit as good as Clark's. Maybe Sean didn't schmooze enough with the powers that be, but he considered it unforgiveable that he hadn't been informed by the company personally of the situation before being blindsided by the partner announcement coming in the mail.

He looked at the screen on his answer machine and saw that the memory was full. He idly pressed the play button to start deleting the messages left by telemarketers during the two months that he'd been gone. He was contemplating taking Maddie to the park before lunch and then to a toy store. Since he saw her so little, he really didn't care if she missed her nap. Given everything that had happened between them, he could care less what Denise would say. She didn't have to know.

Sean was half-listening with one ear to the messages on his answer machine when he realized the message that was playing was from his engineering company. He could hardly believe what he was hearing, and slammed the button on the machine to rewind the tape.

The Brownsdale-Evans Engineering Company is delighted to announce....

Sean's entire body started shaking. He was surprised there wasn't a full page announcement in The Seattle Times. Heck, maybe there had been.

"Daddy, daddy…"

The veins were pulsing in Sean's neck. "Maddie, I need you to be quiet." His daughter was so annoying. It seemed she never stopped whining, and that was Denise's fault. Denise had deserved it when he'd slapped her, no matter what the lawyers had said. It wasn't his fault that when he hit her she'd lost her balance and cracked her skull. It was just an accident that could have happened to anyone.

His mouth was dry, and he swallowed. Pacing the hallway, he shut the door to the living room to block out Maddie's incessant chatter. He needed a few minutes of quiet, so he could think clearly.

Looking down, his gaze rested on the cream-colored envelope. Trembling, he opened the envelope and looked inside. Just as he thought, it was the wedding invite for the Blackstock wedding, which was only a few days away. The reception was being held at one of the swankiest restaurants in Seattle, on the shore of Lake Washington. Sean's mind was working overtime.

He was sure he'd heard someone at work mention that Clark was going to the Cayman Islands on his honeymoon and staying at the Four Seasons Hotel in downtown Seattle in the honeymoon suite on his wedding night. Not that Sean had been interested in the slightest, but recently talk at work of Clark's wedding had been hard to avoid. It seemed like everyone was angling for an invite. It promised to be a prestigious, no expense spared event. It was an open secret that Clark's rich uncle was paying for everything, and that Clark would inherit his estate when he died. Sean had met the shady-looking uncle once, at an office function, when he was introduced to Sean as one of the company's original backers. It seemed to Sean that Clark getting hired by the firm originally, and now this promotion, had the smell of nepotism written all over it. Why couldn't anyone else see what was going on here?

Unbidden, a voice spoke to him in his head. If Clark's uncle died suspiciously, wouldn't Clark become a person of interest in the murder, since he was due to inherit his uncle's estate? Maybe Clark would even be charged with murder and go to prison. Sean smiled for the first time that day.

Actually, that might be arranged, Sean thought, *and then the company would need to fill that partner vacancy. Who better to fill it than someone who had been with the company a long time and who was a pivotal engineer on the company's current premier project?*

He quickly filled out the creamy RSVP card that had accompanied the wedding invitation, indicating he would be attending. He put the card in the envelope provided and walked it out to his mailbox, so the mailman could take it tomorrow.

Maddie was standing in the hallway when he returned.

He gave his daughter a huge smile. "Let's go sweetheart, it's time for pizza."

CHAPTER TWO

"Thanks so much for watching Balto for me today," DeeDee Wilson said as she smiled at her friend, Tammy Lynn. The two women were on the dog-friendly deck at the back of Tammy's coffee shop on Bainbridge Island. "I feel bad about leaving him alone in the house for too long," she continued, passing Balto's leash to Tammy. "As it is, he spends enough time at home alone while I'm working. I'd take him with me, but I'll probably be in Seattle all day."

"Think nothing of it," Tammy said. "We love having Balto here, don't we, Buddy?" She patted her golden Labrador, Buddy. "You run along and catch the ferry. We'll see you later."

DeeDee noticed Balto's ears prick up at the word 'ferry.' The black and white husky looked up at DeeDee with wide eyes, and started to pant.

"Uh-oh. You just said one of the F words. I'd better get out of here," DeeDee said with a laugh. "Ferry and Food. Those are the two words that get Balto excited every time. Would you distract him while I make a run for it?"

Tammy pulled a dog biscuit from her pocket and held it out to Balto. Taking her cue, DeeDee scooted backwards and stepped through the door and back into the busy cafe.

Susie, the waitress, waved to her. "Hi, DeeDee…"

"Sorry, Susie, I can't talk now," a breathless DeeDee replied. "I'm running for the ferry."

Susie laughed as DeeDee disappeared out the front of the cafe in a whirlwind, jumped into her SUV, and sped away.

DeeDee just made it to the ferry terminal as the ramp was about to be hoisted up, and she congratulated herself on not missing the crossing. It was an important day, and she didn't want to be late.

An hour and a half later, DeeDee walked into the Starbucks on Pioneer Square in Seattle. If Tammy's place had been busy, this place was really hopping. With two weeks to go until Christmas, it seemed as if the entire Seattle population had descended on the shopping district and had gone into Starbucks for a morning coffee. DeeDee squinted and peered around the room. She grinned when she saw her sister, Roz, frantically waving from a table in the corner.

Roz stood up as DeeDee approached, and grabbed her sister for a hug. "Careful, you'll squeeze me to death," DeeDee said, laughing. She noted with approval the two mugs of steaming coffee, a plate of chocolate muffins, and assorted cakes which Roz had already bought. "Looks like I got here just in time."

"You sure did," Roz giggled, pushing the plate of treats across the table to DeeDee after she was seated. "Five minutes later and these might have all been gone." Roz said as she stuffed a huge bite of cake into her mouth. "I really shouldn't eat like this," she said, spitting crumbs as she spoke. "But since we're heading to my final wedding dress fitting after we leave here, I figured now's my chance. After today, I'll have to be good until the wedding is over. I don't know how I'm going to survive the next week without chocolate, but I suppose I owe it to Clark to get married in a wedding gown that isn't coming apart at the seams."

"From what I've seen, I don't think Clark would care if you wore a sack," DeeDee said. "That man adores you, but the rest of the three

9

hundred guests might have something to say about it. What happened to the small, quiet wedding you were aiming for?"

"Hmm," Roz said, wiping the crumbs from her mouth before sipping her coffee. "Well, Clark hardly has any family. As you know, his parents are both deceased. He has an uncle that he's close to, and just one cousin of his mother's that he hardly ever sees. Clark being Clark, I thought he wouldn't want to make a big deal out of the wedding, but he said we're only getting married once, so we may as well do it up right. He knew I wanted to have it in the church with the full works, so he said to go for it! Although," Roz said, having the decency to look sheepish, "I may have gotten a teensy bit carried away with it all." She shrugged. "But once the wedding planner Francesca got involved, it took on a life of its own."

DeeDee groaned. "Oh, no. You haven't gone totally Bridezilla on me, have you?"

"Get outta town," Roz laughed. "Apart from it being the most important day of my life, I just want it to be a fun day for everyone else to remember. I knew your catering business would be really busy this time of year, so I didn't want to put any pressure on you, and with me living in Whistler the past few months I couldn't be as hands-on as I would have liked to have been. It just made sense for me to let Francesca do everything. She's been amazing."

"She must be," DeeDee said, "if she was able to arrange to have the ceremony at the Seattle First Presbyterian Church on the Saturday before Christmas, on only three months' notice. That place must be booked years in advance. It's such a beautiful old building, and a great setting for the photographs."

Roz nodded. "I know. I'm not sure how she swung it, and the location in downtown Seattle is great. It's central for the local guests, and close to the freeway for everyone else." She gave DeeDee a pointed look. "I'm telling you, DeeDee, if you ever get married again, Francesca's your Girl Friday. She's taken care of the wedding stationery, the flowers for the church, the photographer, the bridal car, the band for the reception, and probably a hundred other things

I didn't even know needed doing."

"Hold it right there," DeeDee laughed, raising her hand. "I have no plans to get married again any time soon. And as far as I know, Jake doesn't either. At least, not to me, anyway."

Roz frowned. "Everything okay with you guys? I thought things were going well."

"Relax," DeeDee said. "Things are great with Jake, I promise." She thought of her boyfriend of six months, Jake Rogers, and the part he'd played in turning her life around. In the space of a year she'd gone from being a sad and lonely divorcée, to selling the family home in Seattle, moving to Bainbridge Island, starting a new catering business, and falling in love. The realization hit her like a sack of bricks. Her face flushed.

I am in love with Jake Rogers.

"Anyway, this isn't about me," DeeDee said, trying to regain her composure. She couldn't wait to see Jake again, to feel his arms around her, and his lips on hers. "How did you meet Francesca?"

"She came highly recommended," Roz said, giving her sister a suspicious look. "I don't know why you don't want to talk about Jake, but I won't push it. Anyway, Francesca was trained as a CPA like me, so we know some of the same people. I thought since we have a lot in common we'd hit it off, but when I first met her I thought she was a bit of a witch."

DeeDee rolled her eyes. "You're not really selling her to me, Roz."

"It's fine, Sis, she has everything under control, right down to getting the roses for the bouquets dyed the same color as yours and Tink's outfits. The bridal bouquets are winter white orchids with blush roses. Posies for you and Tink, and a cascading arrangement for me. Dyed roses, can you believe it?" Roz laughed and sputtered some of her coffee over her chin before reaching for a napkin.

"Thanks for the restaurant recommendation, by the way. The Catch was a brilliant choice. After the reception, Clark and I are staying at the Four Seasons bridal suite that night."

"And then you're flying to Tuscany on your honeymoon?"

Roz shook her head. "That was the original plan, but December's not the best time of year for Europe. Clark's Uncle Vinny suggested the Cayman Islands. We're flying to Grand Cayman and then taking a boat to a private island. I've been trying to get more information from my darling husband-to-be, but he won't talk." Roz's face fell. "What's wrong, DeeDee? You look worried."

DeeDee was shaking her head. Mentally, she was adding up the cost of the wedding Roz was describing to her, and arriving at a very big number. She leaned in closer to her sister. "Roz, isn't this all going to be very expensive? Of course, it's up to you and Clark what you want to spend your money on, but it's a lot for just one day. It could be a down-payment on a home, or the start of a college fund if you have children in the future. I guess I'm surprised, that's all. It's not like you to be so frivolous with money."

Roz giggled, and her hand flew up to her mouth. "Oh, DeeDee, no wonder you're worried. I'm sorry, I should have told you before. Clark's Uncle Vinny is paying for everything! Isn't that generous of him? We certainly would have had to watch our pennies if he hadn't offered. Clark and I talked it over, and initially I was reluctant, but Clark insisted that Uncle Vinny would be offended if we didn't accept his kind offer." She shrugged. "Uncle Vinny's super rich. What's not to love about that?"

Despite Roz's protestations, DeeDee was still uncertain. Her sensibilities told her that it all seemed very extravagant, but if Roz and Clark were happy with the arrangement, then it was none of DeeDee's business. "If you're sure Clark's uncle can afford it, then yes, that certainly is very generous of him. What line of work is he in?"

Roz surreptitiously looked around several times before answering.

She leaned across the table towards DeeDee and lowered her voice. "Uncle Vinny was in the garbage business." She peered around again to see if anyone had heard.

DeeDee screwed up her face. "Why are you whispering? I hear there's a lot of money in trash. There's no shame in that. Good for him."

Roz burst out laughing. "DeeDee, you are too funny." She leaned in again and raised a hand to the side of her mouth. "I mean, Uncle Vinny was in the Mafia. He's not in it anymore, and now he's a respectable businessman."

DeeDee's face turned white, and her mouth fell open in disbelief. She didn't trust herself to speak, because she suspected there was not a thing she could say to Roz right now that would not offend her sister. The last thing she wanted was for the two of them to argue before the wedding. Roz was staring at her, waiting for her to say something.

"Um, I'm really surprised, that's all," DeeDee said after a long pause. "Clark seems like the epitome of an Ivy League gentleman, not someone whose family is involved in..." It was on the tip of her tongue, but she couldn't get the last part out. *Organized crime.* "How did his family get mixed up in that sort of...stuff?"

Roz took a deep breath. "First of all, this has got nothing to do with Clark, so please don't hold it against him, okay?"

DeeDee nodded. "Fine."

"Vinny grew up in the Cabrini-Green area in Chicago, with his parents and two older siblings, a brother and a sister. His parents were respectable people, but the family fell on hard times when his father was injured in an industrial accident and was unable to work."

"Go on," DeeDee said. She'd heard about Cabrini-Green, which was a notorious example of a public housing project gone horribly wrong.

"Vinny's mother took sewing and cleaning jobs to make ends meet, so she was never home. Valentina looked after their sick father, while the eldest brother, Fonzie, went to community college and worked night shifts in a warehouse. Vinny was fifteen when Fonzie was killed in a fight. He was trying to drag his friend away from a group of thugs who were taunting them. Fonzie was fatally stabbed in the scuffle that broke out."

DeeDee's insides were churning, and a chill ran through her bones. It was easy to make judgments about people, without knowing their story.

Roz continued. "After Fonzie died, Vinny asked a local bar owner for a job. That man was Fingers Gambino, the Don of one of the most powerful Mafia families in Chicago. Eventually, Vinny became a made man. There was finally enough money for his mom to stay home and look after their father and they were able to move out of the projects."

Roz leaned back in her chair. DeeDee knew her sister was watching her intently for some sort of reaction, but DeeDee's face remained impassive.

"Valentina married a Scotsman, and they moved to New York," Roz continued. "Clark's father disapproved of Vinny's type of work, but he understood why he did it. He wanted to be far enough away from Vinny so that Clark would never be exposed to any wrongdoing. Even so, Vinny and Valentina remained close, and Clark grew up thinking the world of Vinny."

"I see," DeeDee said. "Wow. I guess that explains a lot, but how did Clark end up getting transplanted to Seattle from New York?"

"After Clark finished his engineering degree at Yale, paid for by Vinny, a job came up at an engineering firm in Seattle that Vinny had connections with. Vinny arranged for Clark to interview for the position, and the rest, as they say, is history. Clark's been in Seattle ever since. After his father died, his mother moved from New York to Seattle to be closer to Clark. Then when Valentina died, Vinny moved to Seattle from Chicago."

"I have to ask," DeeDee said, "what's Vinny like? Is he scary?"

Roz laughed. "Not at all. You'll like him a lot, I promise. We're all going to dinner on Wednesday night before the wedding, so you and Jake can meet him then."

DeeDee hesitated. "Jake's going to be away with work for a few days, so I don't think he'll be able to make it." She thought that was just as well, as she wasn't sure how she was going to break the news to him that her sister was about to marry into the Mob.

DeeDee mustered what she hoped was a reassuring smile for Roz. "But I'd love to go and meet him. In fact, I'm looking forward to it already."

Even though DeeDee was lying through her teeth, the look of relief on Roz's face was worth it.

CHAPTER THREE

John Denton's chair creaked as he stretched and stifled a yawn. He caught a whiff of his own stale sweat before reaching down to clear a space on the messy desk in front of him, which was strewn with dog-eared files and half-empty Styrofoam cups.

"You want more coffee?" Mike Morelli, John's partner in the Seattle Police Department for the past eleven years, asked as he stood up from his desk opposite John's. "It's going to be a long night."

"Sure. Thanks."

John watched Mike through the dirty glass window of their office as he walked towards the kitchen area. Mike chatted with several people, but lingered at the desk of one of the female police dispatchers. Despite the fact that Mike was married with three children, it occurred to John that his partner seemed to have more than coffee in mind, judging by the way he was flirting with Eileen.

The midnight shift at the West Precinct was quieter now that the seasonal DUIs had been booked. The period before the holidays always saw a new wave of offenders who considered themselves to be above the law. They were mostly professionals who'd imbibed a few too many drinks at the annual Christmas office party and decided to drive home. He was regularly offered bribes to let them off, but John wasn't interested in the money. The only rich police officers he knew were dirty cops.

He'd joined the Department as a baby-faced rookie, the same as his father and his grandfather before him, and considered himself privileged to serve. In four more years, he'd have twenty years of service in, and he'd be eligible for his police officer pension, but John felt like he had more to give. He still hadn't made his mark on the force. He'd made hundreds of arrests, but less than half of those were for felonies, and the rest were for misdemeanors. There were no Distinguished Service medals coming his way any time soon.

Rubbing his unshaven chin, John stared at the piece of paper he'd been doodling on for the past twenty minutes. The name Vinny Santora was the only thing written on it. He scored through the name with three heavy swipes of his pen, then smashed the paper into a ball. He raised his right arm, closed one eye, and aimed at the waste basket in the corner. He let out a loud sigh as he watched it fly across the room before landing on the torn linoleum along with a pile of other paper scraps.

"You need some target practice, my friend," Mike said, entering the office with two cups of coffee. He set one down on John's desk. "Three sugars, just how you like it. How about we hit up the firing range after this?"

John looked up. "Might not be a bad idea. I could do with letting off some steam. Got a lot on my mind right now."

Mike gave him a quizzical look. "What's got you so bothered these days? Oh man, I hope you're not still thinking about Vinny Santora." Mike sauntered over to his desk, shaking his head. "I told you to forget about that guy. We've been over the file a hundred times. There shouldn't even be a file. We've got nothing on him. I'm telling you, John, he's not worth spending your time on."

John opened his mouth to speak, but Mike raised a finger. "Your dad already put the Colonnas to bed. Every possible connection between Santora and the Colonnas is a dead-end. Case closed." Mike wiped his hands in the air.

"I'm not buying it," John said, pulling a well-worn file out of his top drawer. "After the Colonnas were indicted, the prostitution rings stopped for a while. It's just too suspicious that they started up again around the same time as our friend Vinny arrived in Seattle."

John opened the mini-dossier they'd assembled on Vinny Santora and started leafing through its contents. He looked at the photo on the top of the pile. It was Vinny Santora dressed in a cashmere coat and smoking a cigar and had been taken at the Seattle Opera at McCaw Hall, where Vinny was a patron. A slim and tanned silver-haired Vinny was smiling at the camera, his arm around an elderly woman with white hair.

"He's a good-looking guy, you have to give him that," John said, lifting the photo up to Mike. "He probably robbed that little old lady on the way home. Look at that steely glint in those beady eyes of his. I'm telling you, the guy's dirty, through and through. If we can't pin the rackets on him, there's always the murder of Robbie Rivlin."

Mike sniffed and took a loud slurp of his coffee. His gaze followed Eileen the dispatcher, who was walking past the window of the office, before he turned back to John. "That Rivlin guy died in a traffic accident in Chicago thirty years ago. It's a cold case, and anyway, as you well know, it's not in our jurisdiction."

"Yeah, but Rivlin was the man that killed Fonzie Santora in a fight. He went down for manslaughter and was paroled within a few years for good behavior. After that he lived a nice quiet life as a delivery truck driver. Have you ever thought about who might have arranged for the brakes on his truck to fail?"

"This is getting old," Mike said. "From what I understand, it was an icy night, and the brake fluid was leaky." Mike shrugged. "It was probably just one of those things."

John was getting riled. Mike had no skin in the game, but John did. John's father had been the police detective responsible for bringing down the Colonna family in Seattle and getting them put behind bars for multiple life sentences. He wasn't about to let Santora make a mockery of that good work. His father was elderly now and suffering with dementia, but he was still regarded as a hero in the Seattle Police Department. There was even a framed photograph of old Joe Denton hanging on the wall in the lobby of the Seattle Police Department headquarters. John glared at Mike, who rolled his eyes.

"Fine," Mike said. "I'll give you five minutes to run it past me again, or I'm following Eileen into the photocopy room."

John gave a half-smile. "Okay," he said, clearing his throat. "I've been around to the topless bars, making inquiries. They're all run by non-Italians, no Mob connections, and none of them has a police record. The bar managers have never met Vinny Santora, just his right-hand man, Al De Duco. "

"Right," Mike said, looking bored. "So what's Vinny's front?"

"He's been investing in legitimate businesses in the Seattle area for quite some time, is a patron of various charities, and moves in high circles."

"I wonder if he'd like to support the Police Officer's Ball," Mike joked.

"I wouldn't be surprised," John said. "He's probably greasing a lot of palms. There's no wife, children, or other living family members apart from two male relatives. He has a nephew and a cousin."

Mike drained the last of his coffee from his cup. "Is that it? Let's lock him up already."

"I'm telling you, Mike, the bars are money-laundering operations for illegal proceeds from prostitution. Vinny Santora thinks he's above the law, but I wonder why he's making regular trips to the Cayman Islands every few months?"

"Working on his tan?"

John slammed his fist on the desk. "You're not taking me

seriously, Mike, are you?"

Mike stood up. "No, John, and neither will any other law enforcement officer in the United States. Talk to me when you're thinking straight. But I'm telling you," he said, making the shape of a gun with his fingers and firing them at John. "Don't go messing with Santora and expect me to back you up. I'm out."

John watched Mike leave the office and stalk across the room to Eileen's desk.

It's not Mike's fault, John thought to himself. *He doesn't have the calling.*

John narrowed his eyes and squinted at the picture on his desk of Vinny. He couldn't explain it to Mike without sounding crazy, but he knew he'd been chosen as the person to bring Vinny Santora down. It had first come to him in a dream he had over a year ago. His father may have started the work with the Colonnas, but it was up to John to finish it with Santora. The scourge of prostitution in Seattle had to be stamped out once and for all. His dream had been very clear about that.

It had come to him not once, but several times. It was always the same voice and the same vision, and it was always bathed in light. Prostitution was an evil sin of the flesh, he knew that. When he wasn't at work, John could be found at church, praying for the poor souls who had lost their way or been led astray. Whatever the reason for their predicament, John was ready to save them by closing down the prostitution rings operated by people like Santora, and bringing the sinners back to the light.

He knew what he had to do. There was only one possible solution. From his online research, he'd been able to access the social media profiles of Theresa Larkin, the wife of Cecil, Vinny's cousin. John had learned that Vinny's nephew, Clark Blackstock, was getting married locally in a week, and Theresa had very kindly put the venue of the reception on her Facebook page. John had no doubt Vinny would be in attendance.

John smiled, and stuffed Vinny's photo in his pocket, so he could use it for target practice later.

CHAPTER FOUR

"I think I'm going to cry," DeeDee said as she choked back an emotional gasp when her sister, Roz, stepped out of the dressing room in the exclusive downtown Seattle bridal salon of Luly Yang.

They were attending the final dress fitting for the bridal party. Along with Roz, DeeDee and her daughter Tink were also trying on their dresses, so the seamstress could make any needed final alterations.

DeeDee watched Roz glide towards the large full-length Louis XIV style mirror as if she were walking on air. Her sister's dress was breathtaking in its simple elegance. Made from oyster-colored satin, the heavy winter-weight fabric glowed with a pearlescent sheen. A strapless, fitted bodice fell straight across the décolletage, encrusted with pearls and shimmering Swarovski crystals down to the fitted waist. The skirt hugged and accentuated Roz's curves in all the right places, skimming her hips and flaring out toward the bottom. At the back of the dress, the train was several feet long and adorned with the same delicate pearl and crystal hand–sewn jewels as the bodice. A short, open front bolero with cap sleeves in the same fabric, suitable for travel to and from a winter wedding and the church ceremony, completed the outfit.

"You look stunning," DeeDee said wiping a tear from her eye.

Roz screwed up her face as she hoisted the front of the dress up under her shoulders, turned sideways and checked her silhouette in the mirror. Raising her arms horizontal, she started flapping them from side to side. I look like I have bat wings, don't I?" she moaned. "Maybe the sleeves should be a little longer?"

Tink let out a snort, and DeeDee gave her daughter a stern look.

"What?" Tink exclaimed. "Roz, I promise you do not have bat wings. I would be the first to tell you if you did. Mom's just tearing up with happiness. You look so gorgeous, I'd marry you myself. The dress is simply divine. If my dress wasn't so beautiful, I'd be jealous."

Tink shimmied across the room over to Roz, her own dress a blush-colored full-length bias-cut silk slip with shoestring straps. Just as Roz's dress accentuated her voluptuous figure, Tink's complemented her petite frame. Tink lifted a handful of Roz's auburn tresses, which were skimming her shoulders, and bunched them up high above her head.

"Are you having an updo, or wearing your hair down?"

"I haven't decided," Roz said, turning back to face her reflection in the mirror. "What do you think, DeeDee?"

"Up, definitely," DeeDee said with certainty. "With dangly earrings. Are you wearing anything on the neckline?"

"There are plenty of statement necklaces here to choose from," Tink said, her gaze wandering around the room.

The Luly Yang bridal salon was sumptuously decorated with a cream colored carpet and crystal chandeliers. It had the feel of an intimate boudoir, but on the scale of a very grand five-star hotel suite. Around the walls of the room were glass cases showcasing shoes, jewelry, and narrow drawers spilling out delicate underwear fit for a princess.

DeeDee stepped up next to Roz to help arrange her hair, while

Tink wandered over to one of the glass cases. "There aren't any price tags," Tink whispered.

DeeDee grinned at her. "That's because if you have to ask, you can't afford it. There's a good reason why this place is the destination of choice for international A-listers and celebrities. Mere mortals can only dream of owning something from here."

DeeDee's ex-husband Lyle had once bought her a beaded evening bag from Luly Yang's ready-to-wear collection, but that was as far as her Luly experience went. Until today, standing in her made-to-order Matron of Honor outfit, when it seemed like DeeDee's mere mortal dream had come true.

Her reverse silk, sleeveless form-fitting shift dress, in the same shade of blush as Tink's, fell just above the knee, with a coordinating fitted jacket with three-quarter sleeves and one large button in the center under the bust. The two-piece outfit showcased DeeDee's willowy figure to perfection. DeeDee thought she'd never owned anything quite so beautiful, including her own wedding dress. There was no danger of either her or Tink upstaging the showstopper of a bride, but in other circumstances both she and her daughter would easily be in a class of their own at any upscale event.

The ringtone of DeeDee's phone buzzed from somewhere inside the spaciously draped dressing room. She scrambled to find it in her purse, and smiled when she saw Jake's name on the screen.

"Hi," she said, nodding as Jake chatted. The soft lilt of his voice drifted over her, and she lost herself for a moment thinking about weddings, Jake, and what Roz had said earlier that day in Starbucks about DeeDee getting married again. DeeDee had spoken the truth when she said she had never considered it. She would not have allowed herself to believe she would meet anyone who could capture her heart the way Jake had, certainly not after a long marriage and subsequent divorce. But now...

"DeeDee, are you okay?" Jake's voice sounded worried, and DeeDee came to her senses. There must be something about trying on bridal wear that was giving her strange ideas. She didn't want Jake to think she had any thoughts about getting him down the aisle.

"Sure," she said, starting to climb out of her dress. "I'd love to see you later. We're leaving the bridal salon and stopping off at the church before heading to the venue for the reception. We're also meeting the restaurant manager and the wedding planner there later this afternoon. So I guess I should be home by seven tonight."

"Great," Jake said. DeeDee could imagine his smile and his dancing blue eyes at the other end of the line. "I'll cook for you for a change," he went on. "Stop by my place and Balto and I will be waiting. I'll pick him up from Tammy's later this afternoon. I have to go in that direction anyway."

DeeDee said goodbye and finished getting changed, carefully placing her outfit for the wedding onto the padded hanger. Several pins were sticking out where the seamstress was going to make the last adjustments.

She was looking forward to seeing her two favorite guys later, Jake and Balto.

*****

After leaving Luly Yang's, and saying goodbye to Tink who was meeting friends, DeeDee drove with Roz to the Seattle First Presbyterian Church to see where the ceremony would be taking place the following Saturday afternoon.

It had been a while since DeeDee had been there, and she almost choked up with emotion when she stepped inside the majestic old stone building. In her mind's eye, she could already picture Roz walking down the aisle under the vast domed ceiling, her dress shimmering in the afternoon light. DeeDee and Tink would be walking in front of her, with Clark waiting at the altar. As their father had died several years earlier, DeeDee's son Mitch was going to be giving Roz away. If the raw emotions DeeDee felt now just thinking about it were any indication, she knew she'd have to compose herself for the real thing. It was a comfort to know that the three hundred sets of eyes watching the bridal procession would all be focused on Roz, not her.

"This place is enormous," she said to Roz, awestruck. "It's just as well you have so many guests coming, or we'd be rattling around in here." Her voice echoed in the empty church.

"The more the merrier," Roz grinned. "All the better for a great party afterwards." Roz grabbed DeeDee's arm. "Speaking of which, what say we get going to The Catch restaurant? Francesca's probably waiting, and we can get lunch while we're there."

DeeDee marveled at how calm Roz was in the days leading up to her big day. Standing in the church, DeeDee's stomach was full of butterflies, and they hadn't even had the wedding rehearsal yet. That was scheduled for Wednesday night before going to dinner with Clark's Uncle Vinny. The thought of lunch made her hope the butterflies she was feeling were just hunger pangs, and would disappear after they'd eaten.

On the drive to The Catch restaurant, they listened to a radio interview with a local police officer about driving safely over the holidays. Officer John Denton was live on the air, reminding the public to leave their cars at home if they were attending festive parties, and not to drink and drive. "Remember folks, have fun, and be safe out there!"

"What a jerk that guy is. Everybody knows that," Roz said, shaking her head and changing the radio station to something with catchy music. "Turn here, DeeDee, this is the driveway entrance to The Catch."

Michele, the French speaking restaurant manager, greeted them at the door. "Zees way, ladies," he purred, showing them to a table by the window. "Ze wedding planner called to say she will be a little late."

After ordering a glass of wine for Roz, and a sparkling water for

DeeDee—"Officer Denton would be proud," she giggled—Michele sat down with them to finalize the arrangements for the wedding reception dinner, and strongly recommended the restaurant's signature dish of steak topped with grilled mushrooms.

"My mouth is watering," DeeDee said. "Surf and Turf is one of my favorite meals ever. Steak and lobster for three hundred guests will go down in history as an epic wedding feast, I'm sure."

Roz nodded. "That's what Uncle Vinny said," she exclaimed with a smile. "It's expensive, but he wants the meal to be memorable. See, I knew you'd like him!"

DeeDee took a sip of her water. She'd had a few hours for the news about Uncle Vinny's Mafia past to sink in. Somehow it didn't seem real, so she'd decided to put it out of her mind for now. She trusted Roz's judgment, and Roz seemed to like the man. It would be doing him an injustice to form a decision about his character without meeting him. Even so, it was hard for DeeDee's moral compass to contemplate liking someone who was possibly a criminal. Feeling confused again, she tried to push all thoughts about Uncle Vinny to the back of her mind.

Roz finalized the wine order for the event based on Vinny's shortlisted wine choices, which DeeDee noted were flawless. The man clearly had fine taste. Michele left them, and just as they were about to finish a delicious lunch of grilled ahi tuna steak seared black on the outside and red in the middle, cooked to perfection, a scowling woman came rushing over to their table and noisily sat down.

DeeDee looked up in surprise at the rude interruption.

"This is Francesca Murphy," Roz said, with a faint smile. "The wonderful wedding planner I've been telling you about. We know the same people from way back. Francesca, this is my sister, DeeDee."

Francesca greeted DeeDee with a look that was more of a wince than a smile, and gave her a perfunctory handshake. "Pleasure,"

Francesca said, without catching DeeDee's eye.

Francesca proceeded to engage in conversation with Roz, totally ignoring DeeDee during the discussion that followed, which involved various last minute wedding details. DeeDee was happy to finish her meal in silence and simply observe what was going on, although she wasn't sure she liked the wedding planner. Several times, Roz asked DeeDee's opinion on something such as the stationery for the Thank You cards, or gratuities for the wait staff, and DeeDee offered input as best she could. Her ideas were mostly dismissed by Francesca, or met with derision in the form of an eye roll or a scowl.

"One final thing," Francesca said, when it looked like they were wrapping things up. It was getting late, and DeeDee was ready to make her way to the ferry terminal for the crossing to Bainbridge Island, so she could get back to Jake and Balto. "I've received a substantial five figure check from a Mr. Vincent Santora, as a down payment for my services, along with a note to send all of the final invoices to him. Is that correct?"

"Yes," Roz said with a nod. "That's Clark's Uncle Vinny. He's paying for everything."

"I see," Francesca said, sucking in her cheeks. "That's nice. I wish I would be so lucky when I get married."

DeeDee noticed the minuscule diamond solitaire on the ring finger of Francesca's left hand. "Are you getting married soon?" DeeDee asked her gently.

Francesca looked at DeeDee with her signature glare. "Soon enough," she said. "Next Spring. It's a small, private affair. Nothing fancy." After dating her boyfriend Harry for ten years, Francesca had given him an ultimatum, that they either get married without delay or break up. He'd agreed to marry her, but there wasn't much enthusiasm shown on his part. They would be tying the knot at the Seattle Municipal Court with a couple of witnesses, and maybe go for a meal afterwards, just the two of them. It wasn't much to get excited about. "We're paying for it ourselves," she added, with an air of superiority.

"That's lovely," DeeDee said, with a sideways glance at Roz, who was looking bemused. "An intimate wedding is always very special. I hope you and your future husband will be very happy."

"Thanks," Francesca grunted, gathering up her paperwork and standing up abruptly. "If you'll excuse me, I really have to run." With that, she left just as suddenly as she'd arrived.

"Wow," Roz said with a chuckle. "You really rubbed her up the wrong way, didn't you?"

DeeDee shrugged. "That's an understatement. She's very prickly, isn't she? Seems like she has a real chip on her shoulder about your wedding, if you ask me."

Roz tipped her head to the side and thought for a moment. "No, I don't think so. She's just a little shy. Francesca can be a little frosty when she doesn't know people, but we're getting along very well. Honestly, she's fine. You'll see."

DeeDee turned away and waved to the server for the check. Roz didn't have a suspicious bone in her body, but DeeDee wasn't so sure when it came to deciding if a person was on the up and up.

CHAPTER FIVE

"Harry, honey, are you home?"

Francesca put her keys on the hallway table of the small house she shared with her fiancé, Harry Goldsmith. The television was blaring from the living room, but that didn't mean Harry was around. He never turned it off, even when he went out. To do so would have necessitated him to stop for a second and press a button on the remote control handset, which seemed beyond his capabilities. It wasn't that he couldn't do it, he was just too lazy.

Francesca sighed, and picked up a dirty t-shirt that was laying on the floor at the entrance to the house's one tiny bedroom. She could hear water running in the bathroom, and the trail of discarded clothes in that direction indicated Harry was in the shower. She reached down for his jeans, socks, and underwear, and put them in the laundry basket, which was overflowing.

He could do some laundry, it's not like he even works, she thought to herself, sitting on the edge of the bed and taking off her high heels. Ever since the meeting with Roz Lawson and her sister at The Catch that afternoon to discuss Roz's wedding, Francesca had been fuming. Having to deal with clients like Roz Lawson personified everything that Francesca hated about being a wedding planner. Angrily, she threw a shoe across the room. It didn't have far to travel to hit the wall opposite where she was sitting, and it came ricocheting back towards her.

Harry chose that moment to walk out of the bathroom. Wrapped in a towel from the waist down, exposing his dark hairy upper half which was similar to a gorilla, he dodged the flying shoe just in time.

"That almost hit me in the eye," he muttered. "It's about time you got back. What took you so long? I haven't eaten all day. What's for dinner?"

Francesca eyed him with distaste. "Am I to assume the empty potato chips wrappers on the floor in front of the television ate themselves? And the Twinkie wrappers just flew off and fell on the floor as well? That's amazing."

Harry scratched his dark curly hair. He grunted, and started opening drawers. "Where are my clean shirts? The drawers are empty. Some wife you'll make, that's all I can say. I certainly hope you don't think this is acceptable." Then he laughed, and flopped down onto the bed. "Just kidding. Come here, baby, and make Harry happy. You know how much I've missed you all day, don't you, sweetie pie?"

Francesca pushed his eager hands away.

"Get your hairy paws off of me," she said with a shudder. "You're darned right it's not acceptable." She turned and started poking Harry in the chest with her finger. "You need to get a job instead of lying around here waiting for me to come home and cook and clean for you. I'm busting a gut trying to make a life for us. Who pays for everything around here? Francesca Murphy, that's who. Not to mention making all the loan payments on our debts as well. And what thanks do I get? Nada, zero, zilch."

"They're your debts. They have nothing to do with me," Harry said with a diffident shrug.

Francesca glared at Harry, who made a face back, immune to her repertoire of rants. Not succeeding in riling him, she stomped into the bathroom and slammed the door closed. Harry had left a pool of water on the floor, and she cursed as her panty hose got wet. She undressed and turned on the shower. When the steam started to fill the room, she stepped under the warm jets which blasted her from above, and felt the rush of water on her body. Life was so unfair. Francesca had never wanted to be in the bridal business at all. Like Roz, she'd set her sights on becoming a CPA, and went to work for a very reputable company when she finished college.

Unfortunately, one of the partners had been embezzling money from the company's clients for several years and got caught, prosecuted, and sent to prison. The company went bankrupt trying to pay all of their clients back the money the partner had embezzled. After that, she'd tried to make a success by starting her own CPA practice, but after ten years of living hand to mouth she had to admit that her business was a failure, and she closed it. On a whim, Francesca decided to work in a completely new area, and she became a bridal consultant. Attractive, charming, and intelligent, she was able to convince several bridal shops, restaurants, and wedding venues to refer her services to brides-to-be. While her wedding consulting business had become successful, she was still struggling financially to pay back the loans she'd accrued when she had her own CPA business.

Harry yelled through the door. "Are you coming out any time soon? Let's go out for dinner. You'd like that, wouldn't you, honey?"

"You mean YOU would," she screamed back.

Harry Goldsmith was another drain on her finances. She knew they probably would go out for dinner later, and Francesca would pay as usual, since Harry had no money of his own. But without Harry, Francesca had no one. He was the only constant presence in her life. Despite her ultimatum to Harry about getting married, she wasn't sure how she would have coped if he'd decided to break up with her. She didn't want to face life alone.

Apart from Harry, Francesca had no other family and no safety net to fall back on. An only child, both of her parents died in a freak boating accident when they'd been out with friends on their boat. A rogue wave had capsized the boat, and they both died before help could get to them. Fortunately, Francesca's father had been an active member of the local Rotary service club, and Francesca had been the recipient of a Rotary scholarship which allowed her to finish school. Otherwise, her fate could have been even worse.

"I'm sorry, sweetheart," Harry pleaded from the bedroom. "Come out and we'll talk. Come to Harry, baby. You know I love you."

Francesca turned off the water and reached for a towel, but there weren't any. *Harry.* She started to shake with fury. Thinking of her meeting earlier, she would bet the last few hundred dollars in her bank account that Roz Lawson's cute husband-to-be never used the last clean towel. Francesca was sure that wherever Roz lived, there was a never-ending stack of sweet smelling, freshly laundered, soft fluffy towels.

She imagined Clark Blackstock took Roz to dinner at the finest restaurants in town, after she'd finished work in her profitable CPA business. She pictured Roz and Clark discussing their extravagant wedding plans over a bottle of fine wine, and congratulating themselves on their good fortune that their no-expense-spared nuptials were being bankrolled by Clark's rich uncle, Vincent Santora.

Francesca stood shivering and naked in the bathroom, and reached across the basin to rub a patch of steam off the mirror with her hand. She raked her fingers through her tangled, wet locks and regarded her dripping, bedraggled reflection with one part self-pity, and one part self-loathing.

She'd done some research on Vincent Santora when the check he'd sent her arrived, and learned that Clark Blackstock was his closest relative. It didn't take a genius to figure out when Santora died, Clark would stand to inherit his uncle's vast fortune. And Roz Blackstock, as she would be by then, would get an upgrade to her life from perfect to utopian.

Staring at herself in the fogged over mirror, something inside

Francesca snapped as the cold injustice of her situation struck home. She'd been on the same trajectory to a successful career as Roz, except Roz had made it to the top and through no fault of her own, Francesca had not. She wondered how Roz would feel if their situations were reversed.

There was an answer, and it was quite simple. If Vincent Santora were to die in suspicious circumstances, and Clark Blackstock was implicated, her nemesis Roz Lawson/Blackstock's life would come crashing down around her pretty, freckled, little ears.

It would be so good to give Roz a taste of what Francesca had been through. It would be all the sweeter because Roz would have such a spectacular fall from grace. Given the ostentatious wedding she was having, there was no better occasion or opportunity to ruin Roz's future than on her wedding day. Francesca took perverse pleasure in thinking it was fitting that what should be the best day of Roz's life, would end up being the worst. For her part, she resolved to execute a dazzling performance in both halves of it. She would make sure Roz's wedding went off without a hitch, until the tables were turned at the end.

With the decision made, a plot was forming in her mind that made Francesca smile for the first time in a long time.

CHAPTER SIX

Theresa Larkin puckered up her lips and leaned closer to the mirror to apply her bright red lipstick. She made a smacking sound as she pressed her lips together several times before standing back to admire her reflection.

In the dresser mirror she could also see her husband, Cecil, standing behind her in their bedroom. His brow was furrowed into a frown.

"Are you sure that dress is suitable for a wedding?" Cecil asked. "It's a bit revealing."

Theresa smiled sweetly at her husband. "You're such an old fuddy-duddy, Cecil. This dress is perfect for the reception. I have a cape I can throw on for the church. Nobody will be looking at me there, anyway. All attention will be focused on the bride, but this dress will be eye-catching for the reception."

"It certainly will," Cecil dead-panned. He knew better than to argue with his wife. "I just hope nothing pops out of it."

"I will ignore that comment, darling," Theresa said, smoothing the tight skirt of the lace dress over her hips. It may have been a demure gray color, but Cecil was correct that the style was veering toward risqué. With a low, scoop neckline, and sheer gray sleeves, Theresa's breasts were bunched up and heaving over the top of the too-tight fitted bodice. A sparking crystal necklace contrasted with her pale skin and the dark hue of the dress tended to attract even more attention to that part of Theresa's body.

She winked at her husband and continued. "You won't be complaining when you're the one undressing me later."

Cecil's face flushed. "I hope you're not planning on teasing me like that for the rest of the day. You know my blood pressure can't take it." He patted his pockets and fished out a silver foil packet of pills, popping one out and stuffing it in his mouth. "I'm going to get a glass of water. Cover yourself up, woman, or I will have to undress you right now."

Theresa clicked her tongue as Cecil left the room. Her husband was a good man, but he was so dull. He may have alluded otherwise, but the chances of Cecil performing marital duties at any time other than a Friday night after they came home from their weekly date night at the movies, were precisely zero. He showed more enjoyment ravishing a tub of popcorn than his wife.

Flicking her raven mane over her shoulder, the sight of a rogue silver hair in the mirror caused Theresa to lean in and yank it out. She might be looking at forty, but inside she still felt like she was twenty-one and loved to party. Cecil, on the other hand, was ten years older and acted like he was ready for an old folks' home. Theresa was grateful to him for everything he'd done for her, but sometimes she wondered if a life of boredom was worth the trade-off for security. It wasn't even as if they were rich. Theresa had made a big mistake setting her sights on Cecil Larkin rather than his wealthy cousin, but Vinny Santora was out of her league. Cecil didn't mind that her nose was too big and that she had uneven teeth, but she knew her lack of natural beauty wouldn't cut it with Vinny.

Cecil wandered back in. "I heard Clark got promoted at work. Isn't that great? Things are going well for him."

Theresa let out an exasperated sigh. "For goodness sake, Cecil. I

36

could care less that Clark is so successful, marrying a beautiful woman, heading off to the Caymans for their honeymoon, and has a rich uncle who's paying for it all. Is there anything Clark touches that doesn't turn to gold? Because if there is, I'd sure like to know about it."

She lifted her hairbrush and started pulling it through her hair. The scratch of the bristles on her scalp rang through the air. Turning to her husband, she continued her rant. "Run it by me again. I'm having a real problem understanding why you don't care that Vinny is paying for Clark's wedding and is probably going to leave his entire estate to Clark, and not to you. He's going to get all of it, and we're not going to get a dime." She threw the hairbrush down onto the dresser in disgust.

"Theresa, we've been over this before," Cecil said in a patient tone.

"Stop speaking to me like I'm a two-year-old," Theresa said, folding her arms in a huff.

"Then stop acting like one. Clark is Vinny's nephew. I'm only his cousin. Besides, he can leave his money to whoever he pleases. I've told you before, money just isn't that important to me. I've got a nice little job, we've got a house, and we've got Doc."

Theresa threw her hands up in the air. "Yes, we've got Doc! Isn't that just wonderful? Your stupid hunting dog. You love that ugly mutt more than you love me."

Cecil walked over to his wife and patted the back of her shoulder. "Now, dear, don't go getting all upset. You know how I like to go over to the east side of the Cascades when it's hunting season, take Doc, and spend some days in the wild, hunting. I know I'm a lousy hunter. As a matter of fact, I've never gotten a thing, but it's being able to get out of the city and enjoy the great outdoors that makes me happy. I'm glad you thought we should come to Seattle when Vinny left Chicago. I like it here. There's nothing more I need."

Theresa pushed away his hand. "Well, what about thinking of me for a change? I need a lot more. I'd like to buy some clothes at a fancy dress shop instead of searching for bargains at discount centers. I'm getting tired of it, particularly since Vinny has all that money. I don't care if Clark is his nephew, at least some of it should go to you. There's plenty to go around, and I'm going to make sure it does."

"Theresa, I don't like that kind of talk. Vinny's been nothing but nice to us. Remember, he even gave us a toaster when we were married. And it's a four-slice one, at that."

"Are you crazy, Cecil?" Theresa stomped her foot on the floor. "A four-piece toaster gift makes you happy when he's sitting on a boatload of money, and we all know it's probably not of the legal type," she harrumphed.

"Now, now. Don't even go there," Cecil said. "Vinny's retired now. What he used to be involved in is in the past, kind of like what you used to be involved in, I might add." He gave his wife a knowing look.

"You told me you'd never bring that up, Cecil. You promised." Theresa's chin quivered. She had no intention of crying, because it would ruin her makeup, but it was an expression that usually worked to soften Cecil up. "It wasn't my fault I had to work for a while in a topless bar before we met. You know that was a terrible time in my life." She sniffed for good measure.

Cecil dropped his eyes and mumbled. "Sorry."

"As a matter of fact," Theresa continued, "a few of my friends from those days have hinted that your 'retired' cousin isn't actually retired at all, although they can't prove anything. But don't you think it's rather interesting that they all know Al? And Al is Vinny's right hand man? I'd bet everything I own, not that it's all that much, that Vinny is back in his old line of work, right here in Seattle."

It was Cecil's turn to get agitated. As he tried to fasten his cufflinks he said, "You told me you'd completely left that business, and you didn't have anything to do with it anymore. If that's true, how would you know anything about Vinny or what he's involved in these days?"

"Well, once in a while, mind you not very often, I get together with a few of the girls I used to work with for lunch. We talk about old times. The last time we met, the subject of Al and your cousin came up. I thought it was rather interesting, that's all. Actually, I think you should talk to Vinny and tell him we know he's back in the game." She placed her hands on her hips. "Maybe if he knew we're aware what he's doing for a living, he might feel like we deserve a little money. I suppose some might call it hush money, but whatever you want to call it, the color's still green. What do you think?"

Cecil fixed his cufflinks in place and walked over to the closet where his tuxedo jacket was hanging on the outside of the door. "I think that's a subject that is no longer up for discussion. Either in the present or in the future. The answer is absolutely no. Am I making myself clear? Believe me, this is non-negotiable."

Theresa stared at him in silence. Her husband could be resolute when he wanted to be, and she knew there was no point arguing any more about it. She wasn't about to let the matter drop, but she may have to go about it in a different way, that was all. Taking matters into her own hands was a preferable alternative to relying on Cecil to do anything. She decided to play along. "Fine, whatever you say. It's your family, so I'll keep out of it."

Cecil nodded, and appeared satisfied.

"We probably better leave," Theresa said. "Don't want to be late to your cousin's wedding." She opened the nightstand on her side of the bed, took a small pistol out of it, and slipped it in her evening bag.

Cecil wiped his shiny forehead with a folded handkerchief. "Theresa, why did you do that? I didn't know you even had that thing anymore."

"Some habits are hard to break, Cecil. It was a good friend of mine during those years you don't like to talk about. Actually, it saved me several times. I like to have it with me. It makes me feel safe."

Theresa gave Cecil a cold, icy stare, before continuing. "Of course, with Vinny and Al being at the wedding, I probably don't need to worry. If anything were to happen, it will probably happen to one of them."

"Theresa…"

"Oops, sorry." She raised a hand to her mouth. "Silly me. I know, the subject is closed. That just slipped out. Let's go."

Theresa Larkin fastened her cape over her shoulders and flounced through the bedroom door, her husband trailing behind.

CHAPTER SEVEN

"I want you to have this," DeeDee said as she handed Roz a small diamond and silver pendant attached to a blue ribbon with a safety pin. "Mom gave it to me on my wedding day, and it was her mother's and our great-grandmother's before that. Now it's your turn. Pin it inside your bodice so that all of the women in our family can be with you on your wedding day."

Roz's eyes brimmed with tears as she fumbled with the pin, her hands trembling.

"Let me help you," DeeDee said, deftly attaching the ribbon to the inside of Roz's strapless bodice and pushing the pendant under the fabric. "Try not to cry, or you'll ruin the good work that the makeup artist just spent the last hour doing. Now stand back and let me see you before I attach the train to your dress."

DeeDee knew she was chattering, but if she didn't stop talking she was in danger of getting emotional as well, and she was trying her best to keep Roz's nerves at bay. Roz had been so calm during the time leading up to her big day, until she'd awakened that morning at DeeDee's house. That's when the reality of the coming changes in her life had hit.

"Look at the weather," she'd moaned to DeeDee, bursting into her older sister's bedroom shortly after eight and pulling the drapes back. "Wet, cold, and windy. It's a sign. I just know it. Remember when it rained for your wedding to Lyle? And I don't need to remind you how that turned out."

DeeDee rubbed her bleary eyes. "No, but we had twenty or so good years, and two beautiful children, so it wasn't all bad."

"Hmmph," Roz said. "What if Clark and I end up divorced like you and Lyle did? I must be crazy to even think about getting married." Roz was chewing her lip. "I suppose it's too late to call it off now, though. What do you think? Would Clark hate me forever?"

DeeDee had sat up in bed and eyed her sister with a mixture of merriment and concern. "I don't think Clark would ever hate you, but if you really want to call it off, you should. In that case, can I go back to sleep for a little while longer? You can close the drapes when you leave."

Roz had glared at DeeDee and yanked the blankets off the bed, so DeeDee had no choice but to get up. "I guess this means you're going ahead with it," DeeDee had mumbled, before Roz hit her over the head with a pillow.

"The weather forecast is for it to clear up later," Tink said hopefully over breakfast, as the three women sat in silence eating croissants and crispy bacon, watching the rain drizzle down the window panes. Even Balto's mood was subdued. Sitting underneath the table at DeeDee's feet, he made his usual attempt at swiping some bacon, but even that was half-hearted.

"More Mimosas, anyone?" Roz asked as she topped off their orange juice glasses with champagne. The mood in the room had relaxed by the time DeeDee moved the remainder of the bottle to the refrigerator before anyone got tipsy. By the time they'd all showered and changed into the robes that Tink had brought for the occasion, the hair stylist and makeup artist had arrived to start their pre-wedding transformations.

"The rain has stopped," a triumphant Tink announced a little

42

while later, one eye on the mirror and one eye on the window, as the makeup artist applied her mascara.

"You need to stay still, Tink," Nicole, the makeup artist, scolded. "Unless you want me to poke your eye out."

Roz, her hair in curlers, and wearing a white robe that had 'Bride' emblazoned across the back in bright pink embroidery, jumped up and ran over to the window that looked out at Puget Sound. Her face had broken into a smile for the first time that day, and it was at that moment that DeeDee knew everything was going to be fine.

Now, in the room at the church, making the final adjustments to the train at the back of Roz's dress, DeeDee was alone with her sister. When she was done, she stood back for a moment, and thought that her heart would burst with happiness at the sight before her. Roz was the picture of radiance, her natural beauty complemented by her makeup which had been done with a light hand. Her hair was piled loose on her head, several curls escaping at the sides, with diamond chandelier earrings. The tiny crystals and pearls that seamlessly adorned the bolero and the bodice of her dress made it look as if she was shimmering when she moved in the afternoon light. Outside, by some sort of miracle, the clouds had dispersed and the wind had died down. A sense of calm prevailed.

"My baby sis," she whispered, choking up. "I wish our parents were here to see you today." She held out her arm and squeezed Roz's hand, composing herself. She was afraid that saying anything more would open the floodgates, and the two of them would start bawling.

"I know," Roz said, her eyes shining, as if she could read DeeDee's mind. "But you've been like a parent to me, DeeDee, more than you'll ever know. I'll be forever grateful that you're my sister. Thank you."

DeeDee gulped down a sob, half-laughing, half-crying. "I love you Roz, and I am so happy to welcome Clark into our family today. I'm sure you will have a long and happy marriage."

Roz beamed at her, and squeezed her hand back.

There was a knock on the door, which opened just enough for Tink's head to appear around the side of it.

"Jake and Mitch are here," she smiled. Her eyes widened, and her mouth fell open when she saw Roz. "Oh Roz, you look like a million dollars! Quick, give me your phone."

Tink rushed into the room and grabbed the device from the dresser. She pulled the three women together, extending the phone in front of them, and snapped a selfie with her mother and her aunt—all of them grinning ear to ear.

"Are you ready?" DeeDee asked as she smiled at Roz, handing her the cascading bridal bouquet of winter-white orchids and blush roses. "You better be, because it's show time."

*****

DeeDee rested her head on Jake's shoulder as they swayed in time to the music. "I think I'm wrung out with emotion," she said. "Today was perfect. I know I'm biased, but I thought Roz was the most beautiful bride I have ever seen. The look on Clark's face when he was watching her walk down the aisle towards him was a sight I'll never forget."

"You're right," Jake said, his arms around her waist. He pulled her a little closer. "The Matron of Honor wasn't too bad either." DeeDee smiled as Jake lightly kissed her on the forehead. "By the way, I think you have an admirer."

"You mean you?" DeeDee asked as she lifted her head and raised her face to Jake's. She paused when she saw the serious look on his face.

Jake shook his head. "No," he said, staring into her eyes. "Clark's Uncle Vinny. Have you seen the way he's been looking at you all day? He's staring at us right now."

Still dancing, Jake rotated DeeDee ninety degrees, so she could see Vinny and Al seated at a table by the edge of the dance floor. Both men were looking their way.

DeeDee faltered. She'd noticed Vinny's gaze linger on her earlier, when the photos were being taken outside the church after the wedding ceremony, but she hadn't thought anything of it.

"So, what's he like?" Jake asked. "You never said much about the dinner you had with him the other night."

DeeDee frowned at Jake. "I haven't really seen you since you got back from your trip. And it wasn't just me and Vinny at dinner, remember? Roz and Clark were there as well, and Clark's friend John."

Jake smoothed DeeDee's hair. "Shh, it's fine. I'm not accusing you of anything. Vinny, on the other hand…"

"I think you've made a judgment about him ever since I told you about his background," DeeDee said, "and as a result, you've decided you don't like him."

Jake raised an eyebrow. "And you didn't? Come on, admit it. I'm surprised you didn't hit the roof when Roz told you."

DeeDee shrugged. "Sure, I was apprehensive, but as Roz pointed out, Clark was always shielded from that side of Vinny's life. It's my role to support Roz, and from what I can tell, Vinny has been nothing but devoted to Clark, and now to her."

"I knew I should have had Clark checked out before now," Jake said, crinkling his brow. "Then at least we wouldn't have been blindsided by the news."

It was DeeDee's turn to challenge Jake. "Just because you're a private investigator, you can't get your assistant Rob to run checks on everyone you meet." She tilted her head to the side. "Did you have him run one on me?"

Jake grinned. "There wouldn't have been any point. I knew the moment you came to my place that afternoon to inquire about buying Balto, that I had to see you again. Even if you were a felon, I still would have taken my chances on asking you out for dinner, but I had a feeling you weren't."

The music being played by the band had changed to something more upbeat, but DeeDee and Jake continued dancing slowly.

"My feeling about Vinny is that he's not a bad person," DeeDee said. "I may not agree with some of his previous business activities, but since I don't know the details, that's probably all the better. From what I hear, he's out of all that now. I found him to be charming and intelligent company at dinner, but that's as far as it went." She stared intently into Jake's eyes, her lips skimming his. "In case I need to spell it out for you, there's only one man I'm interested in, and it's not Vinny."

"Good," Jake said, his eyes brightening, "because I thought I was going to have to talk with him, and I wasn't looking forward to it."

"Really? To say what?"

"DeeDee, if I thought another man had designs on you, any man, not just Vinny, I would speak to him to ask him what his intentions were. Because, you and me? I'm all in."

DeeDee's heart was whooping inside. "Me too," she whispered, and closed her eyes. Jake's lips met hers, and she lost herself in the moment. Despite all the dancing and partying going on around them, right then she felt like she and Jake were the only two people in the world.

The moment was interrupted by the sound of Roz's voice shrieking in her ear. "Hey, guys, that's enough! Come on," she said, dragging DeeDee away from Jake by the arm. "I'm about to throw my wedding bouquet, and then Clark and I are leaving for the Four Seasons. You lovebirds can smooch to your heart's content after we're gone."

DeeDee turned to grin at Jake who was following along behind. "I think we'll be going soon, too," she said, and Jake nodded in agreement.

The crowd of guests gathered outside the front of The Catch restaurant to send off the newlyweds. Looking around, DeeDee couldn't see Vinny and Al among the assembled group, and thought they must have left already. After what Jake had just said, she was glad she didn't have to see Vinny again, especially if it would bother Jake. She was sure their paths would cross in the future because of Roz, but she'd deal with that another time. Jake's hand laced through hers as she watched Roz turn her back to the bunch of women who had stepped forward, and raise the bridal bouquet in the air.

"Aren't you joining them?" Jake joked. "You might get lucky."

DeeDee looked up at him. "I think I already did."

She turned back in time to see Roz toss the bouquet, which was the cue for several women to scramble forward with their hands waving above their heads. After a mock scuffle, it was a jubilant and giggling Tink who emerged holding the bouquet.

All that was left was for the crowd to throw rice at Roz and Clark as they climbed into the bridal car that would take them to their hotel. When the car drove off, the crowd laughed at the rattle of tin cans hanging off the back of it and the lopsided 'Just Married' sign stretched over the license plate.

"Shall we go?" DeeDee said to Jake, after Roz and Clark had left.

"Sure, I'll get the car," Jake said, walking off.

While she was waiting, DeeDee watched the crowd disperse as many of the guests also began to leave. In the distance, she could see a burly man standing at the edge of the grass, who she recognized as Al. Two things vaguely occurred to her before Jake pulled up in her SUV and she climbed in. The first was that Al was wearing sunglasses at midnight, and the second was that Vinny was nowhere to be seen.

CHAPTER EIGHT

After the bride and groom had left, Al returned to the black sedan with tinted windows and settled back in the leather driver's seat to wait for Vinny. The parking lot was beginning to empty as the guests wandered back to their cars, some lingering to chat with friends. The mood was light, with everyone smiling and laughing. Several taxi cabs pulled up at the front of the building for the people who weren't driving.

Al pressed the button on the dash to change radio stations. That bozo cop was on the radio again, telling people not to drink and drive. If Al had heard the segment once that week, he must have heard it ten times.

"I'm glad the police have their priorities straight," Vinny had commented when the same recording had been aired earlier that day on their drive to the church, and he and Al had both started to laugh. "I guess everyone gets their fifteen minutes of fame," Vinny said when they stopped shaking with mirth. "And Officer Denton just had his. He's a sorry excuse for a cop, if his legacy to the Seattle Police Department is Chief DUI Buster."

"Wasn't his old man the cop that brought down the Colonnas?" Al asked.

"He sure was," Vinny said with a nod. "Old Joe Denton was a

great cop. If there is such a thing." And then they had both roared with laughter again.

Al checked his watch and scratched his head. It had been over thirty minutes since he'd seen anyone leave the restaurant, and much longer from when he had left Vinny inside the restaurant. By now, there were only a couple of cars remaining in the parking lot, and the guests who had been milling around after the bridal party had left were all gone. Al guessed that the cars belonged to people who were leaving them there overnight and had gone home in taxis. He turned off the engine, which had been idling the whole time, and strolled toward the restaurant, his hand on the gun concealed inside his suit jacket. Knowing Vinny, there was a chance he was inside settling the bar tab, and trying to get a discount for paying in cash. The restaurant was totally dark. Al's senses heightened and his step quickened.

Another possibility was that Vinny had been talking to DeeDee, the bride's sister who he'd been very interested in. Maybe he'd gone somewhere with her. But Al was pretty certain that he'd seen DeeDee outside with her boyfriend when the bouquet was thrown, so that theory didn't stack up. His trusty sunglasses had military night vision capability, which was another reason why he rarely had any reason to take them off.

Al walked up to the building and pushed on the closed door. He pushed it again, hard, but it was shut tight. The rattle he heard on the other side of it alerted him to the chains and padlock attached to the door hardware. Taking a tour round the side of the building, he tried a couple of windows and the back entrance, but everything had been secured. His eyes were drawn to the twinkling lights on the other side of Lake Washington, and he headed across the grass to the pier that led out over the water. The only sound he heard was his footsteps on the creaking wooden boards.

A bright moon was visible through a break in the clouds overhead, the water still in the moonlight. Al stopped and looked around, the thud of his heartbeat crashing through his chest. Checking his surroundings from the view on the pier, nothing was amiss that he could see, but the knot in his gut alerted him otherwise.

Retracing his steps back along the pier, he turned where it met the grass of the garden outside The Catch, and walked down the bank to the sand below. As he walked across the beach, he could make out the silver shimmer of a fish bobbing at the water's edge. Walking faster, he approached the object, but stopped abruptly when it became clear that the flash of silver did not belong to a fish. It was the back of a human head.

His natural urge was to run towards the body, but his years in the Mob had taught him to be very cautious. For all he knew it could be a set-up for a hit. He drew his weapon and checked 360 degrees around him to see whether he was alone on the shore. The night vision heat sensors in his glasses confirmed there was no one else there.

It was only then that he allowed himself to run towards the water, wading in up to his knees, and to turn over the body of his lifelong friend and companion, Vinny Santora. The silence was broken by Al's guttural sobs as his body heaved, racked with grief. He carried Vinny's body out of the water as carefully as if it were a glass statue. Vinny's body was cold, the icy waters having accelerated nature's task. Al laid him on the sand, the man he had guarded for over forty years, before blessing himself and starting to pray. Kneeling beside Vinny's body, Al said a prayer that Vinny would rest in peace, and a prayer of forgiveness for himself.

I'm sorry I wasn't there for you tonight, my brother.

Vinny looked like he was sleeping. The only marks on him were two bullet holes in his dress shirt and a small pool of red that had seeped through it caused by the bullets that had killed him. Al pulled Vinny's gun from where it was still nestled in the concealed pocket inside his tuxedo and emptied the contents of his pockets. There were a couple of soggy cigars, a gold lighter, a wallet full of cash, and a business card for a catering company. Then he leaned down and kissed Vinny's forehead, before standing and starting the slow walk back to the car.

He spoke quietly into the microphone in his shirt collar, to let

Charlie know what had happened.

"Vinny's been whacked."

*****

Back at the car, Al placed Vinny's personal effects, together with both their guns, in the glove compartment before calling 911 to report the death of Vinny Santora.

Within minutes the parking lot of The Catch was crawling with police cars and the first of the press corps to arrive. In the distance, Al could hear the sound of a news helicopter before it came into view, hovering above Vinny's body as the police authorities began their investigation.

After explaining to the first responding officer that he worked for Vinny and that they had been attending a family wedding, Al wasn't surprised when the line of questioning started to take a nasty turn.

"Can you tell us, Mr. De Duco, what line of business Mr. Santora was in? And why anyone might want to kill him?"

Al looked blankly at the police officer. "I told ya', I'm not sayin' nothin' without my lawyer present."

"Is it true," the police officer continued, "that Mr. Santora has connections with the Colonna family and the chain of licensed premises known as Tooters?"

Al chewed his gum and stared down at his feet. "Never heard of 'em." His pants were still soaking wet from the knees down, his shoes waterlogged and covered in sand.

"Please remove your sunglasses when we are speaking to you, sir."

Al obediently removed his glasses and placed them in the inner pocket of his suit jacket.

"Let me ask you again, Mr. De Duco, where were you between the time of approximately 11:35 p.m. and 12:45 a.m. this evening, when you found the body of Mr. Santora?"

"Let me tell ya' again, I was right over there, in my car." Al jerked his head over towards where the black sedan was still parked in the same place where he had parked when he and Vinny had arrived at the restaurant. "Only exception was when the bride and groom said their goodbyes. I was standin' at the edge of the crowd with everyone else watchin' them leave."

"Did anyone see you during this time, Mr. De Duco? Do you have anyone to corroborate your story?"

Al exhaled. "It ain't a story. If you want to charge me with somethin' go right ahead. In which case I guess I'll be callin' a lawyer. Till then, you can sit on it."

The police officer started to say something, then changed his mind and made some notes on his pad.

"We're not charging you with anything, Mr. De Duco. For now. But we will be in touch. In the meantime, if you think of anything, please get in contact with us."

"I guess I'll be seeing' ya'," Al said with a nod. He made his way through the crime scene investigators and took one last look at the body of Vinny, lying on a gurney about to be loaded into an ambulance.

Bit late for that, he thought to himself.

Getting into the car and driving off, Al was lost in thought as he sped through the deserted streets. He'd been detained by the police for a couple of hours, not that he was in any hurry to get anywhere. When he finally arrived at Vinny's gated residence, it was after 3:00 a.m.

He made his way into Vinny's office on the ground floor. Turning on the light, he walked across the wood-paneled room to Vinny's desk, where he eased himself into Vinny's chair, before burying his face in his hands. Everything was just so, the way Vinny liked it. There was a neat pile of paperwork on the side of the desk, alongside which sat a well-leafed crime thriller paperback, the genre Vinny loved to read when he relaxed. There were several fountain pens and a small bottle of ink. On the leather desktop were several yellow sticky notes with various scribbles written in Vinny's distinctive handwriting.

Al placed Vinny's gun, wallet and lighter in the top drawer of the desk and locked it. He smiled sadly as he looked at the wet business card in his hand that he'd removed from Vinny's pocket. The card was for Deelish, DeeDee Wilson's catering business on Bainbridge Island. Al placed it beside the sticky note that Vinny had left on the desk with DeeDee's name on it.

He lifted the phone on the desk and made the call he knew the family in Chicago would be waiting for. Charlie would have already informed them of the situation before it hit the network news channels.

"Al," said the voice that picked up. "Sorry for your trouble."

"Thanks Joey," Al said, his voice cracking. "The cops are all over it."

"Little Fingers is sendin' Baby Face out there pronto. He'd come himself, but his wife is about to give birth. She told him if he goes to Seattle he needn't bother coming back."

Al wasn't surprised. 'Little Fingers' Gambino was the head of the family now that his father Fingers was dead, and the only person Little Fingers was afraid of was his wife Elena. "That's okay, Joey. I understand."

"We need to clean up the business, so there's no loose ends. You can show Baby Face the skims and introduce him to the bar managers. We'd still like you on board in Seattle, Al, if that's what you want. Or you can come back to Chicago when the heat dies down."

"I'll think it over. Send me Baby Face's flight details, and I'll pick him up at the airport and arrange a hotel. Vinny's place is being watched." Al didn't need Charlie to tell him that. He'd seen the plainclothes police officers parked across the street from Vinny's property when he arrived at Vinny's house.

The phone clicked dead, and Joey was gone.

Al knew there was no point trying to sleep. Ever since he'd walked into the water to get Vinny, his mind had been working overtime thinking about who could have been responsible. Judging by Joey's reaction, the guys in Chicago weren't expecting Vinny to get hit. For that reason, Al was pretty sure Vinny's death hadn't occurred at the hands of one of the Chicago Mob or even the much less visible Mob presence on their doorstep in Seattle. But if not a Mob member, then who?

Al lifted Vinny's favorite fountain pen and started to scrawl a list of names. He decided if he waited for the Seattle Police Department to catch Vinny's killer, it would be a long wait. There were certain people in the police force that would be glad to see Vinny gone, and one name immediately came to mind. He hadn't mentioned it to Vinny, but that cop on the radio had been sniffing around some of the bars asking a lot of questions.

Officer John Denton

Al was no detective, but in those books that Vinny read he said it was usually someone close to the victim that committed the murder. Family, more often than not.

Clark Blackstock

Al paused, then crossed Clark's name out. He didn't care what the crime books said, there was no way Clark would hurt a fly, never mind his beloved Uncle Vinny.

He tried to remember the name of Vinny's cousin with the awful wife that didn't get along with Vinny. Cecil Larkin, that was it. Cecil was no murderer, but his wife Theresa was bitter and twisted.

Theresa Larkin

There was something else niggling at the back of his mind, a conversation Vinny mentioned to him the previous week. Vinny had lunched with Clark, who said he was having some trouble with a guy at work, and he was regretting inviting him to the wedding. Vinny had been annoyed about it, and said his name was Sean something or other. Al wasn't sure if Sean had any connection with Vinny, but he wrote it down anyway.

Sean ??? - guy at Clark's work

It wasn't a very long list, but Al was sure more ideas would come to him. He wasn't in any hurry. It had taken him ten years after Fonzie Santora died to bring his killer Robbie Rivlin down, and Al was willing to spend the rest of his life finding whoever killed Vinny, if that was how long it took.

He made a mental note to himself to check his offshore bank balance in his Cayman Islands account, since there was a good chance he'd be retiring there sooner than planned.

CHAPTER NINE

DeeDee's arm stretched across the nightstand beside the bed, as she tried to turn off the alarm. She was half asleep, confused, and disoriented. It was only when she realized she wasn't at home, but in the hotel room they were staying in after Roz's wedding, that she knew it wasn't her alarm. Her phone was ringing, and she sat up in bed with a start.

"Roz?" DeeDee said, glancing at the caller ID. She was still groggy. "Is everything alright? It's 5:00 a.m. I thought you weren't leaving for the airport until after breakfast."

Roz didn't speak, and DeeDee wondered if somehow her sister had called her by mistake. Jake rolled over and DeeDee whispered so she wouldn't disturb him. "Mrs. Blackstock, you should be enjoying the benefits of being a newlywed. Go back to bed and call me in a couple of hours. Whatever it is, it will wait until then." She was about to end the call when she heard Roz trying to speak, her voice rasping with sobs.

"DeeDee, please don't hang up," Roz whispered. "Something horrible has happened. Clark's just been taken to the police station for questioning."

Always a light sleeper, Jake had overheard both sides of the telephone conversation, and he bolted up in the bed beside DeeDee. He looked at her questioningly. A stricken DeeDee handed him the phone in silence.

"Roz, it's Jake. What's going on?"

"Uncle Vinny was murdered at the wedding reception. His bodyguard, Al, found him on the lakeshore. Jake, he was shot," she wailed. "I don't know what to do."

"Roz, I know how upset you are, but this is important. Take a couple of deep breaths, and then I want you to tell me everything from the time the police came to when they left. Just take it slowly. Whenever you're ready, I'm here."

Balto had also stirred and came padding across the room from his dog bed in the corner. At home, Balto liked to sleep at the end of DeeDee's bed, but when Jake was there he wouldn't allow it. DeeDee patted the comforter and Balto jumped up on the bed, while DeeDee leaned closer to Jake to try and follow the conversation between Jake and Roz.

Roz was quiet for a few moments, and DeeDee could hear her gulping for air. Finally, Roz was able to continue. "The police knocked on our door about an hour ago. We ignored it at first, and then the knocking got louder. 'It's the police, open up.' they said. 'Clark and Roz Blackstock, we know you're in there.' They made it sound like we were criminals."

"It's okay, Roz, try and keep calm. Go on," Jake said. He looked at DeeDee with a grim expression.

"Clark got out of bed and opened the door, while I put on a robe. Then they told us that Uncle Vinny had been murdered. Poor Clark. He started crying. He couldn't believe it. Neither could I. This is like some kind of a nightmare." Roz began to hiccup.

"When was the last time either one of you saw Vinny?" Jake asked.

"Clark was at the bar with John. Vinny came over and said he was about to leave, and to give me his love, and that he would see us after we got back from our honeymoon. Clark thanked him for everything. Vinny was so good to us. We had a perfect wedding and reception, and it was all because of him."

"How did Vinny seem? Was he anxious or anything like that?" Jake asked.

"No. Clark said he seemed just like normal. He mentioned that Al was waiting for him outside," Roz said as she started to weep again.

Jake rubbed his chin. "I'm curious how the police even knew where you were. Who told them?"

"The police called the manager of the Catch. He went to the restaurant, opened it up, and got out the file on our reception. As the wedding planner, and the person who had made all the arrangements, Francesca's phone number was in it. The police called her, and she told them we were spending the night at the Four Seasons before we left on our honeymoon. Since we were supposed to be at the airport in a few hours, and Clark's been taken away by the police, I guess we won't be going anywhere," she sobbed.

Jake furrowed his brow. "Roz, did the police accuse Clark of anything or give any specific reason why they were taking him to the police station?"

"If you mean did they arrest him," Roz asked, "then no. They said they'd asked the wedding planner if Vinny had been part of the wedding, and what his relationship to Clark was. She told them that Vinny was his uncle. I guess she told them about the toast Vinny had made and the fact that he'd publicly said how proud he was of Clark, and that he was going to be the beneficiary of his estate."

"I'd say you're right," Jake said, pulling back the covers. "Which means that, in their eyes, Clark had a motive for murdering Vinny."

Hardly able to believe what she was hearing, DeeDee followed Jake's lead and jumped out of bed, her heart racing.

"Stay where you are," Jake was saying to Roz, "and don't talk to anyone. DeeDee and I will be there as soon as we can. Should be within the hour. We'll decide what to do then. If Clark gets back before we arrive, let me know. I can imagine how horrible this seems, but we know Clark didn't murder his uncle, and I'll make sure that his name is cleared."

"Jake, he couldn't have killed him. He was with me most of the time from when we walked down the aisle after the minister married us to when the police took him to the station. If he wasn't with me, then there are plenty of people who can vouch for his whereabouts. Please help us."

"I will. We'll be there as soon as we can. Trust me Roz, it's going to be okay."

The look on Jake's face when he ended the call caused DeeDee to believe he was a lot more concerned than he'd indicated to Roz.

"Jake, you don't think that Clark is really a suspect, do you?" DeeDee asked as she pulled on a pair of jeans and a shirt while throwing the rest of her clothes in her suitcase. Her couture matron of honor outfit got stuffed in it along with whatever other items of clothing were lying about the room. Rushing into the bathroom, she grabbed her cosmetics case and ran a toothbrush over her teeth with a lick and a promise.

"I doubt it," Jake said, coming into the bathroom and doing the same. "The police are just starting with the low-hanging fruit, and the person who is going to inherit a wealthy man's estate definitely qualifies as an easy target to throw some blame at."

DeeDee looked at Jake in the bathroom mirror. "There's something else, Jake, isn't there? Tell me what's bothering you."

Jake turned on the faucet and splashed cold water om his face. DeeDee handed him a towel and waited.

"I don't think for a second Clark has anything to do with this, but it would be very convenient for the police to pin this on him. They might try, but I don't think they'll be able to make it stick. But whoever did murder Vinny could be trying to set Clark up, so we don't know what else is around the corner."

DeeDee's eyes widened. "We'd better hurry. Poor Roz must be going out of her mind right now. What a thing to have to go through on the morning after your wedding. No wonder she's so upset." She put her hand on the bathroom counter to steady herself. Jake placed his hand over hers and met her gaze.

"DeeDee, I know you're worried about Roz, and I don't want to alarm you further…but the family she married into—it's a different world than ours. An underworld. The circles that Vinny ran in are full of undesirables. Clark's been dragged into that, no matter how much he was distanced from Vinny's dealings before now." Jake sighed. "I don't want you to underestimate how serious this potentially could be."

DeeDee took a deep breath and smiled up at Jake. "I know you're having a hard time accepting Vinny's past, but what's done is done. Clark's family now. This is Roz's future. Her married life depends on our help. I need to know if you're with me on this, Jake, because I totally understand if you're not. You're the most principled person I know, and I would never hold that against you."

Jake tenderly stroked DeeDee's cheek. "I already told you last night, I'm with you all the way. You can't get rid of me that easily."

"Thank you, Jake," DeeDee whispered, looking intently at him. She had to tear herself back to reality as the urgency of the situation kicked in.

"Time to go, Balto," she called out, slapping her hand on her leg a couple of times. Balto came running over to her. "Jake, I'll walk him around the block while you settle our bill. Meet you at the front door."

Jake nodded. "I'll call the valet now, and they can have our car in front of the hotel after we check out. See you downstairs."

DeeDee opened the door of the hotel room and stepped into the hallway with Balto.

"Oh, and DeeDee?"

She turned to find Jake standing behind her. "Yes, Jake?"

"I love you."

CHAPTER TEN

Less than an hour later, DeeDee, Jake and Balto rode the elevator in silence to the ninth floor of the Four Seasons hotel. A subdued DeeDee closed her eyes and wished she could wake up all over again, but she knew today wasn't going to go away. They had to help Roz and Clark deal with whatever lay ahead. Jake gripped her hand, his hold firm and steady, and she felt some of his strength pass through her. The chime on the elevator dinged and the doors swished open.

"Ready?" Jake asked her.

DeeDee nodded.

At the end of the hallway, the door to the honeymoon suite was opened by a red-eyed Roz, her face puffy and her hair a total mess. She was wearing the robe with 'Bride' emblazoned on the back that Tink had given her the previous morning, however today's version of Roz looked so far different from yesterday's, that she was almost unrecognizable. It was as if Roz had been replaced by an imposter, and her perfect life from the day before had been snatched away along with her essence.

DeeDee took one look at her sister and folded her up in her arms. Roz crumpled into DeeDee, and Jake guided them over to the lounge area of the suite. In other circumstances, DeeDee would have been wowed by the grand scale and opulence of the suite, but at that moment all her energy and attention was focused on her baby sister, Roz. The two women sat on the sofa, with Jake sitting in one of the armchairs opposite them. A round glass and wooden coffee table was in the middle of the seating arrangement, with a fruit basket sitting on top of it.

"It's going to be okay," DeeDee crooned, as she rocked Roz back and forth, the same way she'd always done when Roz was a little girl and had come crying to DeeDee after a childhood tragedy such as falling off her bicycle or when her pet goldfish had died. "I'm sure this is just a huge mistake. Anyone who knows Clark would certainly know he's definitely not a murderer. Everyone can attest to the great relationship he and his uncle had."

At the word 'had' Roz started to howl. DeeDee glanced at Jake, who was rubbing his unshaven chin. If he was uncomfortable at the unfolding scene, he didn't give anything away. DeeDee often thought Jake would make a great poker player due to his gift for maintaining an impassive expression in tricky situations.

Roz's sobs gradually quieted, and eventually she lifted her head from DeeDee's chest and spoke. "I know the police are going to think Clark killed Uncle Vinny for his money. If only he hadn't said in his toast that Clark was going to inherit his estate. It's not as if Clark even wants or needs it." She looked at Jake desperately. "Jake, don't you know someone on the police force? Can't you make this whole thing go away?"

Jake's voice was upbeat and reassuring. "Roz, you know I'll do everything I can. I'm going to go down to the police station and see what I can find out about what's happening. You two stay here, and I'll give you a call when I know something." Jake picked up the car keys for DeeDee's SUV from the coffee table and stood up. He looked at DeeDee and continued, "Make sure you both eat something. I'm not sure how long this will take, but I'll stay with Clark as long as he needs me."

DeeDee was distracted by the sound of her phone ringing, and she mouthed a silent 'Thank you' to Jake as he left. Glancing at the unknown number on the screen, she was unsure whether she should take the call, but something told her to answer it. It was an unusual day, and at times like these, she'd learned to expect the unexpected.

"Hello? This is DeeDee."

A deep male voice with a Chicago accent started to speak. "Mrs. Wilson, ya' don't know me, but please listen to me fer a moment. My name's Al De Duco. Think yer' sister knows me. Anyway, I was Vinny's right-hand man for over forty years."

"Hello, Al," DeeDee said, looking across at Roz. "I saw you with Vinny at the wedding, and Roz explained who you were to me. I'm sure you're as upset as are we."

There was a pause, and DeeDee heard Al take a deep breath before he spoke again. "Ima lot shook up, Mrs. Wilson, and it takes a lot to rattle ol' Al, fer sure. Thing is, Vinny tol' me that you've helped solve a coupla murders. He said ya' were a right smart lady. Think we need to talk and between us, we might be able to find out who killed Vinny."

DeeDee paused. Any assistance they could get to clear Clark's name would be welcome, but the thought of collaborating with a Mafioso was veering into movie territory. And DeeDee knew what happened in those films—a lot of people got killed. A chill ran down her spine. She turned to Roz, who had overheard the conversation.

Roz nodded and whispered, "He's a good guy, just a little scary. He might be able to help us."

DeeDee knew Roz was desperate, and probably wasn't thinking straight. It was up to DeeDee to make a rational decision about how to deal with Al's crazy offer.

"Believe me," Al was saying at the other end of the line, "I'll do whatever it takes to make sure the person who killed Vinny spends the rest of his or her life behind bars, if they even make it to prison." And then he laughed, a low, menacing chuckle. DeeDee heard him make a cracking sound, like bones being clicked into place. Just like the movies.

She made her mind up then and there. "Al, I think time is of the essence. My boyfriend is a private investigator, and he's gone to the police department to try and help Clark. I'm at the Four Seasons Hotel with my sister. Can you meet us here?"

"I'm on my way."

*****

By the time Al stepped into the suite, the sun was coming up. The sky was clear, with no hint of the storm that was brewing inside their lives. DeeDee was standing at the large windows which offered a stunning view of Elliott Bay and Puget Sound, and she turned to greet their visitor.

"Pleased to meet you, Al," she said when Roz introduced him. Al's handshake was strong enough to crush a rock into dust, and DeeDee tried not to wince. "Would you like some coffee?"

Al removed his sunglasses and nodded. "Yes, thank you, ma'am." He wore black jeans, a black turtleneck sweater, and a black wool jacket. He shifted from one leather-soled foot to the other.

DeeDee smiled warmly at him to try and put him at ease. "Please, Al, sit down. I want you to know how much we appreciate your coming over."

The fruit basket on the table had been replaced by a tray of coffee and pastries from room service. The women's hasty breakfast sat unfinished on the dining table in a separate area of the suite. Roz, who had changed out of her robe into the outfit she would have worn to the airport for her honeymoon, if her husband hadn't been detained by the police, poured the coffee.

Al lifted his cup and took a sip, visibly relaxing as he swallowed. He cleared his throat and started to speak. "Think the first thing we oughta do is draw up a list of people who mighta wanted to see Vinny dead. I'm sure ya' both may have heard that Vinny had ties to the Mafia when he was in Chicago."

DeeDee tried to copy Jake's poker face, but she was on tenterhooks as to what was coming next. Al looked Roz right in the eye, then turned to DeeDee and did the same.

Al continued. "That's true. He did have some Mafia connections in Chicago. What ya' might not know is that, and I'll deny this if ya' ever tell this to anyone, he also had some ties to people in Seattle who were somewhat, how shall I say this...let's just call 'em unsavory. That being said, while he may have had some links to 'em, I was the front man for Vinny. None of 'em knew where he lived or anything about his lifestyle, and I'm sure they didn't know about yer' weddin', Mrs. Blackstock."

Roz nodded. "I see. Go on, Al," she said.

"That makes me think whoever whacked him is someone closer to him than one of those people he did business with. I know 'em all, and Vinny paid well. Very well. All of 'em had far more to gain with him alive than dead. I was Vinny's confidante, and he tol' me pretty much everythin'. Mrs. Blackstock, I know how much Vinny loved yer' husband, and I know while the police may be questionin' Clark, I'm convinced he didn't do it."

"He couldn't have," Roz said, her voice shaking. "He wasn't alone the whole time from the moment we said our vows until he was taken away by the police." She blew her nose with what was left of the Kleenex she'd been shredding into tiny pieces the entire time Al had been talking, causing a sprinkle of tissue paper snowflakes to scatter on her lap. DeeDee put an arm around her.

They were interrupted by the sound of the door opening, and DeeDee was relieved to see Clark and Jake walk into the room. A pale, grim-faced Clark sat down next to Roz, kissing her as he did. Jake remained standing, although there was an empty chair next to Al.

"Al, what are you doing here?" Clark asked.

"I'm here to help y'all find who killed Vinny," Al said. "Kinda like maybe we could pool all our information to see what we can come up with. Mrs. Wilson thinks it's a good idea."

DeeDee could feel the heat rising in her cheeks. She didn't need to look at Jake to know his eyes were on her, and she was glad Clark was filling Roz in on what had happened at the police station, so she didn't have to explain herself.

"I've been released on my own recognizance," he said, "but they told me not to leave town. I'm sorry sweetheart, but it looks like the honeymoon will have to be put on hold."

Roz shrugged. "I don't care about that. I'm just happy you weren't arrested. I had visions of you in an orange jumpsuit."

Clark shook his head and reached for Roz's hand. "You know orange isn't my color."

Despite herself, DeeDee smiled and stole a glance over at Jake. His eyes twinkled across at her, and she glanced back at Al who was starting to outline his proposal.

"I think we oughta split up the suspects and see what we got on 'em. It'll go a lot faster that way," Al said. "I gotta coupla names, but maybe you can think of more. Whaddaya say?"

The room became quiet. Roz was looking at Clark, and DeeDee raised her head back up to face Jake. His jaw was set in a straight line, and he was looking at Al.

DeeDee guessed that Jake wasn't thrilled about Al being there, and she couldn't blame him. Since Jake had always been on the right side of the law, as a Marine veteran and now a private investigator, she could understand any reluctance on his part to get involved with Al.

Clark spoke up. "My uncle trusted this gentleman, Al De Duco, like a brother. Al had his back and kept him safe for a very long time."

Al started to protest, but Clark raised a hand to stop him. "Uncle Vinny told me you saved him many times, Al, but he knew that one day his luck would run out. We both know he wasn't afraid of dying. My uncle held you in the highest regard, and his judgment was second to none. I would be honored if you can help us find whoever is responsible for his death." He looked around at the others. "Are we all in agreement?"

Roz nodded.

"Absolutely," DeeDee said. She held her breath, waiting for Jake's response. He met her gaze, and his face softened.

"Count me in," Jake said, reaching across the table to shake Al's hand.

CHAPTER ELEVEN

Al unfolded a neat square of paper with several names written on it in spidery capitals. He looked up at DeeDee, Jake, Roz and Clark.

"Coupla other people here I'll come to in a moment, but first, Mrs. Theresa Larkin. She didn't care for Vinny, and the feelin' was mutual. Do ya' know her?"

Clark and Roz both nodded. "Of course we do," Clark said. "She's married to my mother's cousin, Cecil. I guess he's my only surviving relative now. It's strange you should bring up Theresa's name, because one of the last things Vinny said to me was that he was leaving by way of the garden exit in order to get away from her. He also checked that I had the envelope he gave us for our wedding gift. He'd asked me not to open it until we were on our honeymoon." Clark turned to Roz. "I have no idea what's in it. I didn't even get to thank him properly." Elbows resting on his knees, Clark buried his head in his hands.

"We haven't opened it yet," Roz said, rubbing Clark's back. "Jake gave me a stack of envelopes, and I put them in the hotel safe that's in the closet of our bedroom. DeeDee, could you take a look please? Vinny's envelope is on the top."

DeeDee walked into the vast bedroom of the honeymoon suite and found the safe inside the closet. She didn't need to get the code from Roz, since she knew it would be the first four digits of their mother's date of birth. Sure enough, the door of the safe clicked open when she pressed the final number. Removing a large white envelope from the top of the thick pile of wedding cards inside, she returned to the lounge and solemnly handed it to Clark.

Clark made a rip in the side of the envelope and put his finger inside, tearing it across the top. When he removed the contents, he and Roz both read the words on the grant deed, their faces registering shock as the magnitude of Vinny's generosity sunk in. A speechless Clark, unable to stop tears escaping, roughly wiped his eyes with the back of his hand.

"It's the deed for a house on Queen Anne Hill," Roz gasped, looking up at DeeDee. "This is crazy. We can't possibly accept it." Roz turned to Al for verification. "Did you know anything about this?"

Al's face broke into a wide grin, his gold teeth glinting in the morning sun. "Mighta heard him say somethin' about it on the way to the church. He wanted ya' to have someplace nice to live, somewhere special, for when ya' got back from yer honeymoon and Whistler. Big enough for a family. Ya' gotta take it, ain't no one else gonna get it now that Vinny's gone."

"Sorry folks, I just need a moment," Clark said, bowing his head and standing up.

DeeDee watched a worried Roz follow her distraught husband into the bedroom. The strain of Roz's voice trying to soothe Clark was audible until the adjoining door clicked shut.

Jake eased himself into an armchair close to Al. "Can you deal with the Larkin woman, Al? Not sure DeeDee or I can help you with that one, since we don't know her."

"Ya' got it," Al said, nodding at Jake before glancing back at the sheet of paper in his hand. "Next up's a rogue cop by the name of John Denton."

"You mean the police officer on the radio?" DeeDee said, confused. "But you drove Vinny everywhere. What's the connection?"

"Probably best I don't go into too much detail on that one," Al said after thinking for a moment. "All I can say is, there's history with John's father and some of Vinny's previous associates. I reckon John had a beef with Vinny, that's all. It's been goin' on for a while, based on what I been hearin.' Ima gonna deal with him too."

The bedroom door opened, and Clark and Roz reappeared, hand in hand. They sat back down on the sofa.

"Sorry about that," Clark said, with a tight smile. "This might sound stupid, but there's someone who I think may have it in for me. It's a co-worker of mine by the name of Sean Meade."

"I was just gonna ask you about him," Al said. "Vinny tol' me somethin' about that Sean guy causin' you a bit of trouble. What was that all about?"

"A few people at work mentioned to me that Sean's been bad-mouthing me. Apparently it's because I was made partner when he thought it should have been him. Sean thinks I only got the job at the firm and the promotion because Vinny was my uncle. You see, there's always been rumors flying around that Vinny had ties to the company."

"Vinny invested in that company when it was started, but that's the only part that's true," Al said. "Vinny was real proud of how well ya' always done at work and that ya' made it on yer' own merit. Apart from the original introduction, after that ya' was on yer' own. Haters gonna hate, that's all I can say."

"Sounds like this Meade fellow is definitely worth looking into," Jake said. "Al, you'll have your plate full with the first two. How about I see what I can find on Sean Meade?"

"He's all yours," Al replied. "Ya' got any friends at the Seattle

Police Department, Jake? It'd probably help if we could keep tabs on what their take is on Vinny's murder."

"I sure do," Jake said with a nod. "In fact, my connections there are pretty strong. DeeDee and I were involved with helping them recently on a case when DeeDee's former neighbor was murdered in Whistler. It was a tricky one, but we helped them sew it up. I think our relationship with them is pretty good based on that."

"Rather you guys than me," Al said, folding the piece of paper and putting it back in his pocket. "My feelin' is the cops are gonna concentrate on Vinny's business connections first, rather than personal ones like we're lookin' at. The police are more likely to write it off as an underworld killin' and get back to bookin' DUIs."

Clark spoke up. "Don't forget I'm a prime suspect as far as the police are concerned. They kept going on about me being the last person Vinny spoke to before he left, and that John and I were the only ones who knew he was leaving by the garden exit."

"Were there security cameras?" DeeDee asked Jake. "Surely the CCTV footage will show Vinny and the murderer in the garden."

"That's something I can try and find out from the police," Jake said. "Chances are, the cameras are trained on the building and not the whole garden area. Also, there were plenty of people in and out of those doors the whole evening. Someone could have been lying in wait for him."

"Yeah," Al agreed. He turned to Clark. "When we find out who the murderer is, yer' name'll be cleared. That's the reason we need to act quickly. If the cops can't find out exactly who from Vinny's past killed him, they'll turn their full attention to ya' since yer' his heir. The one thing goin' for ya' right now is that there ain't a solid shred of evidence that I know of connecting ya' to the murder. Everything is circumstantial. But Clark," Al leaned in towards him, "is there anythin' else you wanna tell us? Any skeletons in yer' closet we oughta know about? Because we're all goin' to be somewhat in danger while we investigate this, so best get all the cards on the table now."

Clark shook his head. "Al, there is absolutely nothing. My uncle and I were as close as any uncle and nephew could be. He paid for my college, he was my mentor, and he helped get me my job with the Brownsdale-Evans Engineering Company. He and I talked almost every day, and we met at least once a week for lunch, if not more. Many a time Roz, Uncle Vinny, and I would meet for dinner. As you know, he even came up to Whistler several times to visit us there. He often told me since he'd never been married or had children, that I was like a son to him. He and I were certainly closer than my father and I were, especially after dad died."

Al gave Clark a menacing stare. "What about the money, Clark? Is that why you were so nice to Uncle Vinny, all these years?"

Clark shrunk back in the sofa, and DeeDee gave Jake an awkward look, but Jake was smiling.

"He's just asking you the question the police are going to ask, Clark," Jake said. "It's a reasonable question."

"I know," Clark said, scratching his head. "They already touched on it. The police are going to focus on the fact that I was named as Vinny's beneficiary, but I don't need his money. I'm doing pretty well financially. It never crossed my mind that I'd inherit his estate, although I don't know who I thought it would go to. It just wasn't important to me. First I knew about it was when he announced it during his wedding toast, same as everyone else."

"Nice thought, Clark," Al said, "but not one the cops will pay any attention to. Lemme give ya' some advice. Until this is solved, don't give the police any reason to arrest ya'. I'm serious. Don't even think about speedin' or jaywalkin'. From this moment on, every move ya' make has to be squeaky clean. Got it?"

Clark gave a solemn nod. "Yes, Al. I agree."

Roz tried to lighten up the situation. "I'll try and keep him out of trouble, Al," she said. "I just hope the murderer is found as soon as possible."

"Great," Al said, slapping his hands on his knees. Balto took that as a signal to come over to where Al was sitting. He sniffed Al's legs before nuzzling into him and settling down at his feet. DeeDee smiled to herself. Balto was a good judge of character, of that she was certain. "I reckon that about wraps it up," Al continued. "We need to get started. Is there anyone else ya' can think of who might wanna see Clark, and I should add, Roz, suffer from either Vinny bein' murdered or Clark bein' charged with murder?" He looked around the room. Jake, Roz, and Clark shook their heads indicating no.

Al's eyes rested on DeeDee. "DeeDee, what are ya' thinkin'? Is there someone else we've overlooked?"

DeeDee chewed her lip. "You're very astute, Al. I can see why Vinny thought so highly of you. It's probably nothing, and Roz, I know you're not going to like what I'm going to say, but I think the wedding planner needs to be looked at."

"Are you kidding me?" Roz asked. "I've known Francesca for years. She's not my BFF, but after all she's done for me the past few months, I do think of her as a friend."

DeeDee gave Roz a wry smile. "Sister dear, there's an old saying that I think is apt in these circumstances. It goes something like 'With friends like these, who needs enemies?' Or some such thing. Anyway, I have a completely different take on Francesca." She turned to Al. "I think Francesca's terribly jealous of Roz, and although I'll grant you that this is a stretch, she could be resentful enough to commit murder."

"DeeDee, that's the craziest thing I've ever heard. Why would you even say something like that?" Roz asked, her voice raised.

"I think," DeeDee said, "you were so excited when the two of you were planning your wedding that day I met her that you didn't notice several things. Remember how she made a nasty comment that it must be nice to have a rich uncle, and how she and her boyfriend were getting married, but they were paying for it themselves?"

Roz shrugged. "Are you sure you didn't take a dislike to her because she wasn't very friendly towards you? I told you, she can come across as aloof, but it's because she's shy."

"Hmm," DeeDee said raising an eyebrow. "That's an understatement. Okay, let's look at it another way. You've told me she didn't make it on her own as a CPA, and she became a wedding planner after that failed. You, on the other hand, have a very successful husband, and more business of your own than you can handle. Francesca had to hear that at some point your husband was going to inherit a lot of money, plus she was already aware Vinny was paying for all the wedding and honeymoon expenses. Don't you think that could have grated on her?"

"She knew about the house as well," Al interjected. "I was with Vinny when he mentioned it to her the day of the wedding. From what I saw, she had a gripe about somethin' fer sure."

"It's probably worth checking her out," Jake said. "It sounds like not only did this woman have a motive, jealousy, but she was well positioned to move in and out of rooms and could easily have left the restaurant for a while."

"Yer' sayin' ya' think this woman murdered Vinny?" Al asked.

"No," Roz said. "No way. If it makes you happy, check her out if only to eliminate her, but I'm not going to have anything to do with it. She would never forgive me."

DeeDee had always admired Roz's fierce loyalty to her friends. However, she thought in this case Francesca didn't deserve it, but there was no point arguing about it any further. "Tell you what," DeeDee said. "I've met her, and I'll see what I can find out about her. Roz, I know she's too close to you. I promise I'll be nice. Okay?"

"DeeDee, we've had this conversation before. I'm not real crazy about you talking to someone who could be a murderer," Jake pointed out.

"Well, I'll tell her that Tink caught the bridal bouquet, which she did, and she's thinking about getting married. I can say that I'd like to talk to her about possibly being the wedding planner, since she did such a good job on Roz's wedding. I'll ask her about fees, and all that stuff. I'll be nothing more than a potential client. That make you feel better, Jake?"

Jake grunted. "A little. As long as I know where you are when you meet her."

"Reckon we should all find out what we can as soon as possible," Al said, "then meet up again to see what we got. Vinny's place is under surveillance already. Any ideas?"

"How about the Starbucks on Pioneer Square?" DeeDee suggested. "Jake and I live on Bainbridge Island, and I'm sure you don't want to spend the time taking the ferry over there. Since Clark can't leave town, the police may also be watching his house. Let's meet late tomorrow afternoon, say at 4:00? That will give us today and tomorrow to see what we can come up with."

"Sounds good," Al said as he stood up and walked over to the door. His new best friend, Balto, followed him. Al turned to Clark and said, "Vinny woulda wanted ya' to be cleared of any wrongdoin'. More than anythin'. I'm kinda lookin' at this as the last thing I can do for him. You'll be exonerated, kid. That I promise." He raised his eyes to the heavens. "I made a vow to Vinny, and we keep our vows." With a nod, he crouched down and petted Balto before walking out the door.

The others looked at each other, and Jake was the first to speak. "I feel like I've just gotten in bed with the devil, but a nicer devil, you couldn't hope to meet." He laughed and winked at DeeDee. "This goes against everything I've done since I got out of the Marines, partnering with a Mafioso. Clark, my man, I hope you're worth it."

For the second time that day, DeeDee's heart soared. She knew the reason the very ethical man she was in love with was doing all of this was because of her. Relaxing for the first time in several hours, she sensed Jake watching her. She had a feeling he also knew what she was thinking.

CHAPTER TWELVE

"I feel better than I did on the way up," DeeDee said on the ride back down in the elevator. "This whole situation is awful, but now at least I know we're doing something about it. Vinny was lucky to have a friend like Al on his team." She moved closer to Jake and kissed him lightly on the lips. "And I'm lucky to have you on mine."

"You'd do the same for me," Jake said simply. "I know you were reluctant to leave Roz, but there's really nothing we can achieve by sitting in the hotel all day. Since it's Sunday, I'm afraid that Sean Meade may go back up to Whistler tomorrow, or even this afternoon, and I'd like to talk to him before he goes. Would it be okay with you if I leave you and Balto off at the ferry, and you can get a taxi at the other end?"

"Sure," DeeDee said. "In fact, I could do with a long walk anyway, to try and clear my head and make sense of all of this. I'm sure there will be no complaints from Balto, right?"

Balto raised his head and started to pant.

"I guess there's your answer," Jake said, grinning. "I also want to talk to my contact at the Seattle Police Department and see what I can find out about Sean Meade. My contact can also probably tell me if the police are trying to build a case against Clark, or if they're following a different line of investigation. How about if I invite myself for dinner tonight, and we can share notes and decide what we're going to do. Sound okay to you?"

"Sure. I'll come up with something for dinner for us."

"Somehow, I never doubted you would," Jake said.

They walked out through the lobby in silence. DeeDee thought she saw a few of the staff whispering as they passed, but she ignored them. She guessed the police raiding the honeymoon suite in the middle of the night, followed by an early morning visit from the scary looking Al, had started the rumor mill.

In the car she returned to the conversation they'd started in the elevator. "I know how crucial timing is on something like this, so I think it's important for you to you try and talk to Sean, if you can. I imagine Francesca, the wedding planner, is taking today off, but I thought I'd call her and see if I can set up an appointment for tomorrow. What do you think?"

"Sounds good," Jake said, weaving the car through the quiet Sunday streets. "I also need to call Vinny's contact at the engineering firm where Clark and Sean work. Maybe he can tell me something about Sean, although that will have to wait until tomorrow."

When they arrived at the ferry terminal, there was a long line for the next crossing. Jake jumped out and opened the doors for DeeDee and Balto. "You'll be able to get on since you're foot passengers," he said, watching DeeDee clip Balto's leash to his collar. "I'll be over about seven tonight. I also want to spend some time this afternoon with my assistant, Rob, and see what he can come up with by searching the Internet."

"Great. See you later," DeeDee said, kissing him goodbye.

Jake bent down and held both sides of Balto's head with his hands. "Balto, watch DeeDee for me."

The big dog looked at Jake as if he knew exactly what he had been told, and had every intention of doing Jake's bidding.

*****

Jake had called Rob after dropping DeeDee and Balto off, and asked him to get an address for Sean Meade. He got a cup of coffee to go and took a walk on the waterfront while he was waiting for Rob to get back to him. Rob had been working with him for several years, ever since Jake had opened his private investigator business, and Jake felt very fortunate to have found him. Nothing that Jake asked was too much trouble for Rob, even on a weekend.

"He lives in Kirkland," Rob said when he phoned back, and read the details to Jake. "He's a bit younger than Clark, and he's been working with the Brownsdale-Evans Engineering Company for ten years or so. From what I could find out, he's generally highly regarded by his co-workers and the company. He's a senior project manager and next in line to be a partner in the firm."

Jake had no idea how Rob could find out things like that on a Sunday when the company was closed, but Jake had yet to see where Rob had made a mistake in the information he was able to obtain, often on very short notice.

"Thanks Rob," Jake said when he'd written down the address. "Is there anything else I need to know?"

"I thought this was interesting," Rob said. "He split from his wife a while back after she filed a complaint against him alleging domestic violence. The complaint was later withdrawn, and no charges were brought against him. He's been attending anger management counseling as part of the divorce mediation process. He has one daughter, pre-school age. He's been working in Whistler on the same ski lift project as Clark, and he sees the kid when he's home, which isn't that often."

"Great, thanks Rob. I'm heading there now," Jake said, ending the call and turning back to where he'd parked his car.

Jake easily found the address Rob had given him, and pulled up to the curb next to a real estate 'For Sale' sign. Sean's home was in a residential neighborhood, and although the house looked a little shabby from the front, Jake thought it just needed a coat of paint and some maintenance to tidy it up. Children were playing in the street, and he heard a dog barking from a nearby backyard.

A car was parked in Sean's driveway, and although the shades on the front windows were down, the sound of a television blasting from inside indicated that someone was probably home. Jake rang the doorbell, and heard footsteps in the hallway. A moment later the door was opened by a good looking man wearing a Seahawks t-shirt and gray sweat pants. Jake thought he looked to be around forty, maybe a little younger.

"Can I help you?" the man asked Jake, quickly turning his head back to hear what had caused the crowd on the television to roar.

"Hi, I'm Jake Rogers. I'm looking for Sean Meade?"

"That's me," Sean said.

"I'm sorry to bother you and take you away from the game, but if you have a couple of minutes, I'd like to talk to you."

The man hesitated. "May I ask what this is about?"

"Yes. You may have heard that a man by the name of Vinny Santora was murdered at a wedding reception last night. I understand that you were at the wedding and the reception. It was for Roz and Clark Blackstock. I'm a private investigator, and I've been hired to help find out what happened. I promise, this won't take long."

Sean opened the door. "You're in luck, Jake. That was the last play of the first half, so come in and we'll talk during the break." Jake followed him through the hallway into the living room, and Sean motioned Jake over to a chair.

"I don't know anything about a murder taking place," Sean said when they were seated. "Yes, I was at the event, but I left kind of early. I've been here for about a week, and I'll be going back to Whistler after the game. We've gotten a break on the weather, so our engineering team is going all out until the snows come, and we have to halt the project until spring."

"I see," Jake said. "Sean, I understand that you work with Clark Blackstock. Can you tell me something about your relationship with him?"

"We've been co-workers and friends for more than ten years, which was when I started with the company. Our friendship got waylaid recently, I'm sorry to say."

"Why was that?"

"I've had a lot of stuff going on in my personal life. What with Clark making wedding plans and me in the middle of a divorce, it was difficult for me to stomach his happiness. Then I found out last week that Clark had been made a partner at the company, and I kind of lost it, I'm afraid." Sean gave Jake a rueful smile. "That's something I'm working on, my quick temper. It's gotten me in a lot of trouble in the past."

It struck Jake that Sean seemed like an upfront kind of person. "Sorry to hear that."

"I found out about Clark's promotion by mail," Sean continued, "when I got back from Whistler. My mail had piled up, and I was going through it. I was really angry when I found out about it, and I simmered for several days over it. I finally decided I might as well find out why I hadn't been notified as a courtesy, and I called the senior partner of the firm, Ted Brownsdale." He looked over at the television to make sure it was still half-time.

"I found out the whole thing was a big foul-up. There's a few other things I could call it, but given I've just met you, I'll leave it at that. Ted had called me at my number in Whistler, and left a message that he was naming Clark as a partner, and to let me know I was next in line on the partner list, but they thought I wasn't quite ready yet. He said he wanted me to know about it before I read it or heard it from another source."

"Well, that doesn't sound like a mix-up to me," Jake said.

"The problem was, I wasn't in Whistler. I was here, taking my first break in months. Ted had instructed his secretary to have notices of the new partnership sent to all the stockholders, of which I'm one. That's how I found out."

"I can certainly see why that would make you angry."

"You have no idea. I was ready to do anything I could to disparage Clark and make him pay for it. Once I got an understanding of the whole picture, I was going to tell him all about it at the wedding and apologize, but I never had a chance."

"Sean, I hate to ask this, but can anyone corroborate what time you got home last night?"

Sean was silent for a few moments, and then nodded. "Monica, the woman who lives next door can. She's going through a divorce as well, and we get together when I'm in town, if you know what I mean. We're kind of friends with benefits. Last night was one of those nights."

They both heard the knock on the door, and Sean got up to answer it. "Good timing," he said. "Monica said she'd be over for the second half of the game, and we could spend a little time together before I leave for Whistler. You can ask her yourself."

Jake heard the door open, and Sean returned to the living room followed by an attractive redhead.

"Monica, I'd like you to meet Jake Rogers," Sean said. "He's going to ask you a question, and I want you to answer it truthfully."

Monica turned to Jake and gave him a dazzling smile. "Hi Jake.

What would you like to ask me?"

Jake looked at her clear green eyes, flawless complexion, and couldn't help but notice she had a body that was perfect. "Monica, could you tell me what time Sean came home last night?"

Monica looked at Sean, and her face flushed. She turned back to Jake. "He was here about 9:30 p.m. I asked him why he'd come home early from the wedding, and he told me he wanted to spend as much time with me as he could, since he was leaving for Whistler later today."

Observing the body language between Sean and Monica, Jake thought it was time to make himself scarce. "Thanks to both of you," he said, standing up. "I'll get out of your way." He glanced at the television, where the game was just starting up again. "I'll be rooting for the Seahawks. Don't worry, I can let myself out."

On the way back to his car, Jake made a mental note that they could cross Sean Meade off the suspect list. *One down*, he thought, *and several to go.* He wanted to call Ted Brownsdale the following day just to sew up loose ends and confirm Sean's version of events, but from what he'd just seen, he was satisfied Sean was definitely not the murderer.

CHAPTER THIRTEEN

Located underneath a freeway viaduct, Al entered a dark, unmarked bar called Paulie's Place, which opened at 8:00 a.m., even on Sundays. Busy with patrons from the neighborhood who worked all hours, Al knew many of them had stopped in for a beer before they'd even made it home after their night shift.

He walked over to the bartender, nodding to a few regulars he recognized. "Rick, I know it's Sunday, but I'm wonderin' if Sid's in his office."

Rick pushed a beer across the scarred bar towards Al. "Nah. His kid's in a martial arts competition over in Spokane this weekend. He won't be back until tomorrow. Anything I can do for you?"

Al knocked back the beer in four gulps, and let out a satisfied sigh. He set the empty bottle down on the countertop. "Theresa Larkin," Al said. "Name ring any bells? Think she mighta' worked here pole dancin' a few years ago. Heard she was pretty good. I need some information about her."

Al followed Rick's eyes to where a half-naked pole dancer was doing her moves for the early Sunday morning drinkers sitting at tables around the small stage. "Inez knows her," Rick said, nodding towards the gyrating woman with one leg around the pole and the other high in the air. "I heard her talking about Theresa just a while ago. I think they still meet up pretty regularly. If you want to stick around and talk to her, Inez will be on her break in a little while,."

"Sure," Al said, "I'll wait. Hit me up with another beer, will ya? Night I've just had, I need it."

Rick did as he was directed, and Al sat on a bar stool, nursing the bottle. "Know anythin' 'bout a cop named John Denton?" Al asked. "Has he been in, by any chance?"

Rick shook his head. "No, but I can ask around if you want."

"Yeah," Al said, watching Inez finish her set and accept tips from the onlookers which they gave to her by stuffing cash into the side of her scanty underwear. "That would be good, thanks."

There was a smattering of applause before Inez started to walk to the curtain behind her.

Rick did a piercing one-handed whistle, and Inez turned around. "Man here to see you," Rick called across to her, gesturing towards Al.

Inez lifted a short robe from the side of the stage and pulled it on while she walked over to where Al was sitting. She removed the dollar bills from her thong and counted them quickly before stuffing them into the pocket of the robe. Sitting on the bar stool next to Al's, she allowed her robe to fall open.

"Well, hello sailor," she whispered, biting her lip. "I think I've seen you in here before, but never had the pleasure of meeting you."

"The pleasure's all mine," Al said. He took in her peroxide blond hair, the thick layer of makeup, the tattoo on her shapely breast, and thought there was probably a nice woman underneath it all, but she'd definitely seen better days.

"Are you going to buy me a drink," Inez purred, "or just sit there staring at me all day?"

"Best bottle of champagne ya' got for the lady please, Rick," Al said, never taking his eyes off Inez.

"Maybe we should go in the back," Inez said, tracing her lips with her tongue. "I have a room where you'll be a lot more comfortable. A fine strapping man like you buying little ol' me champagne deserves more than a bar stool." She folded her legs in her best impression of Sharon Stone. "What do you say, big boy?"

Al knew the drill, since he was the one who wrote it. He recalled instructing Rick, as well as all the other bartenders in Vinny's bars, that when a man wanted to buy a drink for one of the dancers, to make them pay top dollar for the best booze in the house. The bars always kept a few bottles of eye-wateringly expensive champagne in stock for just that purpose. It was up to the women to take it from there, but they were all professionals and knew how to get the most money from a man that they could.

"I'll tell ya' what," Al said, while Rick poured the champagne. "Why don't we just talk instead? I need some information, and I think ya' can help me."

Inez's eyes narrowed. She let her smile drop and pulled her robe across her chest, securing it tightly at the waist. "You a cop?" she sneered, lifting her fluted glass and slurping the bubbles. "You don't look like one, if that's any consolation."

Al smiled and adjusted his sunglasses. "Thanks," he said. "I ain't no cop. But I understand ya' know a woman by the name of Theresa Larkin, used to dance here. Would that be correct?"

"Yes, we get together for lunch from time to time. What about it?"

"She workin' these days?" Al said. He nodded to Rick to keep Inez's glass topped off.

Inez shook her head. "She was a lot more fun before she retired. Says her husband told her she can't work in a place like this anymore, because his cousin wouldn't approve of it. I never heard anything so stupid. She's a grown woman, and she should do what she likes. I mean, what the heck is that all about?"

Al was amused at the irony of Theresa saying she couldn't work in a bar like this because of what Vinny would think, since Vinny was the person who owned it. "That's a shame," Al said. "What does she do now?"

The champagne had loosened Inez's tongue, and she seemed quite happy to share the details of Theresa's latest exploits with Al. "Funny you should ask, since she just called me this morning. Said she'd been at a wedding yesterday. Had a great time, so I hear."

"Really? Why was that?" Al inquired.

"Well, it wasn't all good, because she found out her husband wasn't going to inherit a dime from his rich cousin, but I don't think that was totally unexpected."

"Hmm," Al said. "So what was the good part?"

Inez laughed. "You obviously never met Theresa. She was excited because she got to sit next to one of the groom's clients, a very wealthy shipping company owner who was having the groom's engineering firm tear down and rebuild his office building that's located right on the waterfront. Said it was a highlight of her life, to be around that kind of wealth. She even got to ride in his fancy car."

"Maybe she's in the market for a new husband," Al observed.

"Maybe she is, maybe she isn't," Inez said with a shrug. "She's allowed a bit of fun, why not? She sounded bitter about the cousin's money but resigned to the fact that apparently the bridegroom was the person who was going to get everything."

"Can you remember the name of the man who was the shipping magnate she befriended?"

Inez's eyes widened. "Of course. It's only Dino Argyros! He's in the papers all the time. Everybody knows his name."

Even Al was impressed that Dino, a friend of Vinny's, had taken her for a ride. Maybe Theresa was upping her game. He took out a wad of notes and peeled off a hundred dollar bill which he handed to Inez. "Thank ya'," he said, before standing and straightening his jacket.

"Won't you stay a while longer?" Inez pleaded with him. "I don't often get to chat with men who don't have their dirty hands all over me. It's a nice change."

"Some other time, maybe." Al nodded at Inez, gave Rick a half-salute and walked out of the bar.

Outside, he called Rob, whose number Jake had given him, and asked him to get a cell phone number for Dino Argyros. Jake had told all of them if they needed information on someone, Rob was the one who could get it. Al noted it didn't take long for Rob to call him back with the number. Dialing it, the call was answered on the first ring.

A Greek-accented voice spoke. "This is Dino."

"Hey, Dino. Al De Duco here. I'm callin' about the weddin' reception you was at yesterday. My boss, Vinny Santora, was the man who was found murdered outside the reception area late last night. He was also Clark Blackstock's uncle. I'm helpin' the police and could really do with a quick word in your ear, Dino my man."

"Of course, Al. I don't think we've ever met, but Vinny and I go way back. I was shocked and terribly saddened to hear the news this morning. Vinny will be missed in the business community."

"Yeah, tell me about it," Al said. "Listen, I'll get straight to the point. Did ya' notice anythin' at the reception? Anyone actin' suspicious or weird?

"No, I don't think so," Dino said. "But then I wasn't really looking. The conversation at dinner was rather lively."

I'll bet it was, Al thought to himself. "Where was ya' sittin', and who else was at yer' table?"

"I was at a delightful table near the door to the garden. My seatmates were the Larkins, the Brownsdales, Cassie Roberts and her two grown-up children, and some other friends of the bride. I can't remember their names. Theresa Larkin was bending my ear most of the night, but she was good company."

"I hear she can be the life and soul of a party when she wants to," Al said dryly.

"Actually, come to think of it," Dino said. "There's something I should mention. I didn't think much of it at the time, since a lot of people carry guns, but given the circumstances, it might be relevant."

"Someone had a gun?"

"Yes. I was telling Theresa I'd just bought the new Bugatti Chiron, and that it had cost over three million dollars. She asked if she could see it when I was leaving. She wouldn't take no for an answer, to be honest. She put some lipstick on just before we went outside, and I noticed a gun in her purse."

Al let out a low whistle, which was more because of Dino's car than the fact that Theresa had a firearm. "Do ya' know what kinda' gun it was, Dino?"

"I'm a gun collector, so yes, it was a .22 pistol. I asked her about it, and she told me she always carried a weapon. Said she'd had some problems several years ago, and it made her feel safer when she had it with her."

"That's understandable, I guess," Al said. "So, when ya' gave her a ride in yer' car, where was her husband?"

"Oh, he was waiting. Pleasant guy, didn't seem to have much of an interest in cars. Theresa and I went for a spin, and then I dropped her off at her car and went home. I did wonder why she and her husband followed me out of the parking lot and down the street for quite a ways, but I soon outpaced them."

"I see. Listen, Dino, really appreciate all yer' help. I'm tryin' to get information on everyone who was there, and I'm gonna follow up on Theresa, although the murderer coulda' been someone else."

"I hope you find the person, Al," Dino said. "I will be steering clear of Theresa Larkin, in any case."

Al hung up and pressed another number on his phone. "Jake? It's Al. Do ya' know what type of gun was used to kill Vinny?"

"No, but I'm on my way to the Police Department to meet a friend of mine, so I'll see what I can find out," Jake said. "Why do you ask?"

"Because according to Dino Argyros, Theresa Larkin was packin' a .22 pistol," Al said, "but I don't think she did it. She went fer a ride with Dino in his new car, and then he saw her and her husband leave together. She woulda had to leave him, shoot Vinny, and come back in cool as a cucumber. I jes' don't see it happenin' that way."

"I agree that it sounds unlikely," Jake said. "I just met Sean Meade, and think we can rule him out as well. There are a few more things I want to find out, so I'll fill you in tomorrow."

"Sure," Al said, walking back to his car. "I've got several more visits to make myself."

CHAPTER FOURTEEN

Three dive bars and two hours later, Al showed one of his bar managers, Bill Lewis, a picture on his phone of John Denton from his professional profile page on LinkedIn.

"Ya' know this guy, Bill?"

"Let me see that," Bill said, taking the device from Al and squinting at the handset through his horn-rimmed glasses. "Yes, he comes in here from time to time." He motioned to a table in the corner. "Let's go sit down."

Al followed Bill through the crowded bar to a table that was empty due to its obscured view of the stage, where two topless dancers were strutting their stuff. "The dancers look like they're gettin' younger, Bill," he said when they were seated. "Ya' sure they're not underage?"

Bill, a collegiate-looking young man wearing a casual shirt and chinos, shook his head. "No way. I check all their paperwork myself."

"Good," Al said, nodding in approval. Vinny had told Al to always hire managers that looked as squeaky clean as possible, and Bill looked the part as well as being smart. The policy was one reason why the bars' illegal activities had pretty much gone unnoticed by the

Seattle Police Department. Al drummed his thickset fingers on the tabletop. "So whaddaya know about this cop, John Denton?"

Bill tilted his head to the side while he thought for a moment. "As I said, he comes in every now and then, and sits at the bar with a Coca-Cola. He keeps his back to the stage when there's a performance on, but the rest of the time he looks around a lot, like he's trying to memorize people's faces. Not the girls though, he never looks them in the eye. He's kind of, holy I guess, to put it nicely. He talks about religion a lot."

"So he's not leerin' at the girls, and he ain't doin' shots. Do ya' think he's jes' snoopin' around?"

Bill made a face. "He did ask one time about who owned the bar, and I said that you give the orders, like you told me to. He seems weird but harmless. Bit crazy if you ask me."

"In what way?"

"Like he's trying to save people. Says he hears voices. He once told me the reason he doesn't drink is that one day when he was drunk he'd heard a voice telling him to give up alcohol. The voice had said his father wouldn't be proud of him, and his wife was getting ready to leave him if he didn't give it up. Said he was pretty sure the voice had come from..." Bill raised his eyes, "up there. Ever since then, not only has he never had another drink, he's become very active in a church not far from his home."

"Do ya' know where he lives?" Al asked, slicking his hair back with his palm. "Think Ima gonna pay John a visit."

"No, but he prays at The Living Light Church. I remember the name, because he told me he'd be happy to take me if I ever wanted to go. Someone there might know where he lives."

"Bill," Al said, standing up. "I'll take it from here. Keep up the good work, son. You'd better get back behind the bar, those girls are makin' the drinkers work up a thirst." He slapped Bill on the back as he passed the younger man's chair, and squeezed his burly frame through the customers standing four deep near the stage.

Outside in his car, Al called Rob and asked him if he could get a residential address for John Denton. Rob impressed Al yet again by calling back with the address within minutes. Al figured it was a pity he hadn't known about Rob when Vinny was alive. They could have made good use of a man with Rob's skills.

It was a leisurely drive to the address in Renton, about eleven miles southeast of Seattle. As well as being home to John Denton, it was also the home of the Boeing empire. Al could see that while parts of the town were in the process of being gentrified, the address that Rob had given him for John was in a lower middle-class neighborhood that looked to be a ways from gentrification.

Al found the house easily. John's place was the same as all the other one story homes on the street, except for the pink balloons and streamers hanging from the doors and windows. The big pink sign hung on the garage, "Welcome Home, Baby Sarah," looked like it was brand new. Al parked on the opposite side of the street, and as he was getting out of his car, a man came out of the house next to where it was parked.

Al greeted him, and tipped his head toward the sign. "Is there some kinda party goin' on? I stopped by to see John Denton, but I don't wanna interrupt if they're havin' a bash."

The man stopped and smiled. "John and his wife just had a baby girl, last night."

"Oh, I didn't realize that, or I woulda' brought a gift."

"They're still at the hospital," the man beamed. "Baby Sarah was two weeks early. The Dentons attend the same church as our family, and everyone is so happy that John and his wife's prayers have finally been answered. They've wanted a baby for a long time."

"That's real nice," Al said. He was a sucker when it came to babies. He thought of them as cute little cuddly things with gummy smiles. They got him in the heart every time. "Is it The Living Light Church that ya' go to? I ain't been down there for a while."

"That's right," the man said. "I hope you don't mind me saying so, but I can tell you're troubled."

"Really?" Al said. *If only you knew how much*, he thought to himself.

The man reached across to Al and squeezed his arm. "You know, you'll always be welcomed back into the fold. Don't be afraid, my friend, to ask for forgiveness. Redemption is always there for the taking."

"Thanks," Al muttered. "But I think it might be a bit too late for me. When's the family expected home? I should come back with a card and a teddy bear fer the little one."

"It's never too late," the man said. "John reached out for help when he needed it and look at him now."

"Yeah, I've been hearin' him on the radio. He's kinda famous, I guess."

"That's not what's important. John is surrounded by love. When Mrs. Denton went into labor, John was so happy to share the news. He called several of his friends to tell them, and they all met at the hospital to support him. It was a long, hard labor, but Baby Sarah was born last night, around 10:00 p.m., and John's been at his wife's bedside the entire time."

Al tapped his foot. "So when did ya' say they were comin' home again?"

"They should be back later his evening. All the church members are going to be here with food and presents when they arrive. Even Pastor Brian."

"I see," Al said. "That's kind of him, seein' as how Pastor Brian must be a busy man and all."

The man nodded solemnly. "He is. Between you and me, he might not stay long, but he kind of has to stop by since John is a reverend in the church now."

Al scratched his head. "Well. There ya' go. I guess I'll come back a little later then. Good to meet ya', er…"

The man beamed an evangelical smile. "Gary. I hope you will remember what I said."

"I sure will, Gary, and thanks." Al jumped into his car and drove away with a screech of tires. Mentally scratching John off the list of suspects, he turned the car in the direction of home.

For Al, home was a separate guest residence on the grounds of Vinny's mansion, but now that Vinny was gone, he knew it was time to make his own arrangements for the future. He had a few ideas going around in his head, but his main priority was finding Vinny's killer.

With Vinny dead, there were still a lot of people he needed to call in Chicago. He wondered if Vinny's attorney, Dom Langello, knew about his death, and decided to get in touch with him in the morning. His own personal affairs were pretty straightforward, and could wait until after that.

CHAPTER FIFTEEN

DeeDee kicked the sand with her bare feet as she unclipped the leash from Balto's collar and let him run loose on the beach.

"Don't go too far," she called after him, her hands cupping the sides of her mouth to make the sound of her voice travel farther, but it was lost on Balto, a combination of the husky's speed when off leash and the bracing December wind.

When DeeDee and Balto had arrived home earlier that afternoon, the sight of the wedding paraphernalia from the day before had set DeeDee off into a flood of tears. There were florist buckets on the porch where the bridal bouquets and the buttonholes for Jake and Mitch had been stored in water until they all left for the church, unwashed champagne flutes from when they'd made a toast to Roz before she left the house to become a married woman, and DeeDee and Tink's robes with a flash of pink on the back saying Matron of Honor and Maid of Honor, respectively. That Roz's special day ended with the murder of Uncle Vinny was inconceivable, and the thought of Clark being charged for his murder even more so. But it was a real possibility.

She had to get out of the house and clear her head, and the beach was her favorite place to do so. She watched Balto running in and out of the waves, then speeding towards her and turning in the other direction when he got close and veering back off into the distance.

"If only real life was as simple as yours, Balto," she said, throwing a stick for him to fetch. Her face and eyes were salty, a combination of the sea air and her tears. Balto approached her with the stick in his mouth and dropped it at her feet, but before she had a chance to throw it again, he was distracted by another dog on the beach and raced away.

DeeDee strolled toward where Balto had started to play with a German shepherd puppy. He was showing the puppy the water, going in for a paddle and waiting for the puppy to catch up, then following the puppy out again every time it ran off, frightened by the waves. DeeDee smiled at the puppy's owner, a man in his twenties, but she wasn't in the mood for making small talk with someone. She sat in the sand and traced shapes with the stick, trying to make sense of the events of the day.

Attempting to think of reasons why Vinny was murdered was making her head hurt, and after a while she let her mind become idle. If she'd never met Vinny, but had seen on the news that a mobster had been murdered, she didn't think she would have cared. But meeting Vinny had thrown her preconceptions upside down, and DeeDee was having a hard time matching up the person she'd met with the dead mobster on the television. And as for Clark, his pain was obvious to see. She knew Jake was right and that staying at the hotel with Clark and Roz would have been futile, but all the same, she felt bad about leaving them. She decided to call Roz when she got home.

DeeDee closed her eyes and let the gentle soothing sound of the waves wash over her. She understood Jake's affinity with the ocean, and she admired that he swam most days in the Sound, year-round. DeeDee was strictly a fair-weather swimmer, and she'd agreed to allow Jake to give her surfing lessons when the weather improved in the Spring. Her fiftieth birthday was coming up soon, and the thought of learning to surf was both liberating and terrifying to her.

A wet, panting, lump of black and white fur lay down on the sand beside her. "Have you had enough, Balto?" she smiled, opening her eyes and rolling Balto onto his back for a belly rub. The afternoon light was fading, and she noticed they were the only figures left on the beach. "Has your pal gone home? Time for us to go too, and see what we can fix for dinner."

Back at the house, DeeDee washed the sand off Balto's paws. When she'd finished, he padded over to the refrigerator door and waited for her. DeeDee laughed and opened the door. "I know dinner's on your mind, Balto, but I've already decided what we're having. Let me just check to make sure that I've got everything."

The weather had turned cold and the thought of a stew felt warming and comforting under the circumstances. After peering inside the refrigerator to confirm that there was enough meat to make a stew, she closed the door. Along with a tossed salad and some French bread, she should be good to go.

"Hey, Roz," she said softly into the phone when her sister answered her call a short while later. "I've been thinking about this, and I'm feeling really positive about it all. With Jake and Al on Clark's side, he's got nothing to worry about. I'm sure the mystery of who killed Vinny will be solved within a day or so, and then you can go on your honeymoon."

Roz sounded somber, but not tearful. "I hope so, Sis. Clark's going out of his mind. We called the hotel in the Caymans, and they can still accommodate us in the honeymoon suite even if we have to delay the trip for a few days, since they don't have any other bookings."

"That's something at least. What about the airline?"

"I spoke to them myself and explained we missed the flight due to a death in the family. They said their policy is that they will waive the transfer fee and to call them when we know what the revised schedule will be."

DeeDee tucked her feet underneath her legs on the sofa. "And what's the situation with Clark's work?" she said. "Can they do without him for a while longer if necessary?"

"Clark spoke to his boss, Ted Brownsdale, at home. Clark told him what had happened and Ted said that because of the lack of early winter snows, the project is actually ahead of schedule. So if Clark is gone a few more days than planned, that should be fine. Oh, and DeeDee?"

"Yes, Roz?"

"I know we're all meeting at Starbucks tomorrow afternoon, but could you and Jake come to Clark's condo afterward for dinner, and bring Balto? We're using it when we come back to Seattle from Whistler."

"Sure," DeeDee laughed. "You know Balto loves any excuse for a ferry ride. I can see his ears pricking up right now. Any particular reason?"

"I'm trying to convince Clark we need to get a dog," Roz said.

"Oh you definitely do," DeeDee replied. "Everyone needs a dog. It should be the law. I think that will be fine with Jake, unless something regarding Clark comes up."

Roz hesitated. "How's that going? Have you heard anything?"

"I told you not to worry. Jake and Rob, plus Al, are all working on it right now. See you tomorrow, Roz. And take care of that husband of yours."

"Thanks, DeeDee, see you tomorrow."

While she had the phone in her hand, DeeDee decided to call Francesca to leave a message about arranging a meeting.

"Hello, is that you, Francesca? This is DeeDee Wilson, Roz Blackstock's sister."

"This is she," Francesca said. "Hello, DeeDee."

There was an awkward pause. "I'm sorry for calling you on a Sunday," DeeDee said. "I expected to get your voicemail."

"I need all the business I can get, so my phone is on 24/7. How can I help you?" Francesca's tone was businesslike.

"My daughter is getting married next summer," DeeDee lied. "She loved everything you did for Roz's wedding yesterday, so much that I was hoping to arrange a meeting to talk about hiring you to help plan her wedding."

"Oh, congratulations!" Francesca trilled. "You must be so excited, DeeDee. Tink looked beautiful yesterday. I'm sure she'll be a radiant bride on her wedding day. I would be delighted to be of service in any way I can."

DeeDee marveled at how the dollar signs in front of Francesca's eyes had given her an instant personality transplant. "Could we meet tomorrow?" DeeDee asked. "I'd like to get the ball rolling before the holidays, if possible, and that doesn't leave much time."

"No, it doesn't." Francesca sighed. "I could probably squeeze you in."

"That's very kind of you," DeeDee said. "I'll be in downtown Seattle tomorrow afternoon. How about one in the afternoon at The Girl and the Fig restaurant. Are you familiar with it?"

Francesca replied that she was, and when the appointment had been confirmed, DeeDee got up to fix dinner. Just as she was putting salad plates and forks in the refrigerator to chill, she heard a knock on the door.

"I always know it's you when Balto goes running to the door," she smiled, letting Jake in.

Jake opened his arms, and she buried herself in his embrace. She could have stayed like that for a very long time, but she figured he was probably tired and hungry, so she peeled herself away and led him by the hand to the great room.

"I see you got the fire going," Jake said as he walked over to the wood burning stove to get warm.

DeeDee handed him a glass of wine, "Think we could both use this after today. Any luck this afternoon?"

"Thank you," Jake said. "I spoke to Sean Meade and a woman called Monica, who he said he spent last night with. He left the wedding early and Monica is his alibi. Apart from me checking a few details with his boss tomorrow morning, I think we can pretty much rule him out."

DeeDee took his coat. "Sit down, you look exhausted. What did Rob find out?"

Jake sank into the sofa, and rubbed his forehead. "Rob found out quite a lot about everyone, but I'm so tired, I'll just tell the whole group about it when we meet tomorrow." He gave her a weary smile. "I hope you don't mind."

"Of course not. And Al?"

Jake raised his eyebrows. "No idea. He won't return my calls. I know he called Rob several times with requests for phone numbers and addresses, but apart from that I have no clue what's going on with him."

"He's probably grieving." DeeDee sensed Jake's frustration. "I think Al needs to feel that he's doing something for his old friend. Forty years is a long time to be with someone. It must be like the end of a long marriage."

Jake took a gulp of wine and stared straight ahead. "I guess I wouldn't know about that, because my marriage sure didn't last that long."

DeeDee observed Jake in silence. She'd never seen him like this before, and thought maybe her choice of words had been unfortunate. "I…"

"I'm sorry," Jake blurted out at the same time.

She leaned across and kissed him. "Let's have dinner."

"What's in the stew?" Jake asked, when he was on his second helping. "I love it."

"Ah, that must be my secret ingredient," DeeDee smiled, watching him eat. "It's barley."

"Barley? Are we on a health kick or something?"

"The barley helps to thicken it," DeeDee explained. "And since you mentioned several times you'd like to lose a few pounds, I figured you could do without a noodle or rice base for the stew."

Jake sucked in his belly and sat up straight. "In that case, since I've been so healthy I guess I could justify dessert. Do you have any?"

DeeDee smiled and cleared the dishes. "I'm glad you asked, as there's something I've been wanting to try. Promise you won't laugh."

"I never laugh when it comes to food," Jake said solemnly. "Isn't that right, Balto?"

"How does this sound? Nutella on warm French bread. I read an article about melting chocolate and combining it with butter to put on bread, but I thought Nutella would even be better."

"I guess we could try it and see what it tastes like, and Balto agrees. Look DeeDee, he's wagging his tail."

"It looks like you're not going to get any complaints from him," DeeDee said, as she started to prepare the dish.

"No complaints from me, either," Jake said when he'd finished, pushing his plate away. He reached across the table for DeeDee's hand. "I'm sorry about earlier," he said, looking into her eyes. "It's been a long day, and I have a feeling tomorrow is going to be eventful as well. I don't want to, but I should probably go soon. I'll take Balto out for a walk before I leave."

"It's okay," DeeDee said, squeezing his hand. "I know the feeling. I'm almost asleep on my feet. Do you mind if we go for dinner to Roz and Clark's tomorrow after our meeting at Starbucks? Roz wants us to help convince Clark they need to get a dog."

"I think that's a good idea," Jake said. "Some sort of normality to take all our minds off…well, you know."

"The fact Clark might be charged with murder?"

Jake nodded gloomily and said, "I think we'd better call it a night."

CHAPTER SIXTEEN

Al eyed the suitcase and the few boxes he'd spent the early hours of the night before packing in the cottage he lived in on the grounds of Vinny's house. He wasn't exactly sure what was going to happen today, but as soon as it did, he knew he had to be ready. His finely tuned instincts usually warned him of an imminent threat, except when it had let him down the night Vinny died. He knew he'd never forgive himself for that, and had no intention of trying.

He opened the ancient laptop Vinny had given him when he'd upgraded to a shiny notepad electronic device that was about as thick as a sheet of paper. Al never had been able to understand how so much technology could be squeezed into something so small.

"It's called microchips, Al," Vinny had tried to explain to him. "They can package computer circuitry into tiny pieces of silicon and make them do amazing things. It's fascinating. Bill Gates was telling me about it one time."

"I don't trust them things," Al had grunted. "Only chips I use are at the casino."

Al never sent emails, but his sister emailed him photos of her grandkids and wrote him news about what was happening back home in Chicago. The only other thing he ever used the computer for was to check his offshore bank account in the Caymans. When he booted it up and went to the site, he found he had more than enough money to live a very comfortable life there for the rest of his days. He was actually looking forward to living in his beachside home, drinking some Tortuga rum, reading, and finally losing himself into anonymity.

Al turned off the laptop and placed it in the top of the suitcase that contained everything he could possibly need. He was used to traveling light. In his line of work it was sometimes necessary to disappear on short notice, and as a result, he'd never been one to accumulate many material possessions. Family and friends were the most important things to Al, and Vinny had been his best friend as well as his employer. Al wasn't sure if Vinny had known he was like a kid brother to Al, but he suspected he did. Al had taken on that role when Fonzie Santora had died, and the dynamic relationship between the two of them had remained for the next forty years.

He sniffed, and rubbed his eyes, looking around for his sunglasses. It wouldn't be good for anyone to see him with red eyes, as if he'd been crying. Al's tough guy persona was something he'd perfected over the years, and it had become like an armor to him. If anyone knew how much he loved watching The Sopranos in his pajamas with a tub of Ben & Jerry's ice cream, they might not be so scared if they met him in a dark alley.

He remembered the time he and Vinny had lived in Mexico for a year after an investigation by the Feds for tax evasion. Vinny had learned to speak fluent Spanish and Juanita, their housekeeper, had taught Al to cook. Al's salsa dancing had improved a lot too. That was the last time he'd had anything approaching a real vacation, and he wondered if the Caymans would be quite as much fun.

Only it won't be the same without Vinny, he thought.

He'd replayed the events of Saturday night over and over in his mind, trying to think how Vinny's murder could have been prevented. Al would happily have given his own life to go back to Saturday night and save Vinny's.

Checking the time on his Ballon Blue de Cartier watch that had been a gift from Vinny, he decided it was time to make the call. It was after 9:30 a.m., and he was sure Dom Langello's law office would be open for business by now. Dom was Vinny's attorney, but he didn't take regular clients. There were only a few select individuals and businesses that he worked for exclusively and only on a retainer basis. His executive assistant put Al's call through to him immediately.

"Hey, Dom. Ya' heard about Vinny?"

"Yes, Al," the Italian accented voice said. "Please accept my condolences. Vinny was a true gentleman. I, for one, owe him a great debt of gratitude, and I'm sure I'm not the only one."

Dom had all the requirements necessary to be an admired attorney in Seattle, including the Yale law degree, the house in Medina, and memberships in the Sand Point Country Club and Seattle Health Club. No one knew that Vinny had taken a kid out of Chicago, paid for him to go to Yale, and persuaded him to practice law in Seattle rather than in his hometown when Vinny had moved there.

"Yeah, the feelin's mutual," Al said. He heard Dom shuffling papers.

"I was getting ready to call you. All I know is what the news says. Give me your thoughts. Think it's a business deal?"

"My hunch is, it ain't business," Al said. "But I'm still workin' on it. My concern is what's gonna happen to the business. I thought Vinny was gettin' ready to wrap it up before all this happened. He told me he'd had enough. Did he say anythin' to you 'bout that?"

"Yes," Dom said. "But first let's talk about Clark. I heard a rumor his neck's on the block. There were some unverified reports on the news that Vinny mentioned in his wedding toast that Clark was the beneficiary of his entire estate, and that Clark could get charged with the murder. That's certainly true about Vinny's last will and testament, but it's not that straightforward."

"What's the issue? I heard Vinny say with my own ears that Clark was gettin' the lot."

It sounded like Dom was tapping a pen on his desk. "I'm not sure if anyone knows this, but there's a contingency in Vinny's will that if Clark is convicted of any wrongdoing, Vinny's estate goes to his cousin, Cecil Larkin. I'm afraid you have me to blame for that," he said.

"Jeez," Al said, scratching his head. "The way things are lookin', ol' Cecil could be winnin' the jackpot. I'm sure his wife, Theresa, will be happy about that."

"You know how it is," Dom said. "In circles like ours it's pretty easy for a person to be persuaded or influenced to run afoul of the law. Vinny was adamant Clark should never follow that path. That's why I suggested putting the contingency in, just in case."

"It makes sense," Al said. "Let's just hope we can get Clark off the hook."

"Al, Vinny said you were taken care of. You going to be okay?"

"You betcha," Al confirmed. "Vinny paid me plenty over the years, an' I always tol' him, don't ya leave me nothin', Boss." Al twisted the large diamond ring he wore on the pinkie finger of his right hand, another gift from Vinny.

"Okay, good to hear that. Now then, the topless bars. Clark knows nothing about them. Since Vinny was getting ready to retire, he recently transferred them into a company owned indirectly by me. According to Vinny's instructions, the company will sell the bars and donate all proceeds to a charity of my choosing. He said he'd gotten tired of all the dirty business over the years."

"That's why I was his front man," Al said. "He was easin' himself out even then. With the prostitution rings disbanded and the bar proceeds goin' to charity, maybe that was his way of atonement."

"You could be right, Al. Vinny was a generous man. He told me Clark was going to be getting more than enough from his will and that he wanted me to take care of the other money. Also, he decided it would probably be just as well if Clark didn't know about it, so he can't be tainted by the bars in any way. Shame he's tainted by this murder business, though."

"My lips are sealed," Al said. "And will ya' quit goin' on 'bout Clark and the murder? Ima take care of that. Clark didn't kill his Uncle Vinny no more than I did. The real culprit's gonna be found soon. I got a feelin' in my bones about that."

"I know your intuition is probably what's kept you alive this long, Al, so I'll tell you what. I'm going to hold off probating the will until the murderer is caught, because I don't want to have to do it twice."

"Good idea. If I have my way, you won't have to wait too long, Dom. I'll be in touch when I've got somethin' to tell ya. And Ima call Joey and tell him the bars are to be sold, and he don't need to send Baby Face out here."

"Fine, Al. And good luck. I hope to hear from you soon," Dom said, ending the call.

As soon as the call ended, Al sprang into action. After loading his suitcase and personal boxes into the trunk of his car, he made his way to Vinny's office on the ground floor of the main house. He needed to make sure if the police searched Vinny's personal and financial records they'd find nothing to link him to the Mafia, topless bars, prostitution rings, or anything else Vinny had been involved in over the years. Locking himself inside the office, he shredded documents, files and even photos of Vinny playing golf with the Colonnas and Gambinos.

Several hours later when he was finished, he'd made sure that whoever searched Vinny's home would find nothing but the papers and personal effects of a man who liked to play the stock market, watch his investments and his bank account, listen to Spanish for Beginners CDs, and read Lee Child novels

CHAPTER SEVENTEEN

DeeDee checked her phone messages and returned some of her calls. With just over a week to go until Christmas, her catering business, Deelish, was already booked solid, and she was surprised that so many people had left it to the last minute to organize their catering arrangements. It was unfortunate she had to let people know she was not available, however there was one message that made her pause.

The female voice on the answering machine was instantly recognizable, before the woman even said her name.

"Hello, Deelish! My husband has been very naughty and invited some people over for New Year's Eve without telling me. It's just going to be a teensy weensy little party. Maybe fifty people. I know it's the very last minute, but you simply MUST cater for us. I've heard so many great things about Deelish, and no one else will do. I'll simply die if you can't do it. Please, please, pleeeeeease call me back as soon as you get this message. Money is no object. Bye. Oops, it's Dana Donnelly, by the way. Call me. Bye! Bye, bye, bye." DeeDee smiled. She thought she heard a 'mwah' at the end of the message, like someone kissing down the phone.

"Dana D!! Oh Balto, do you know what this means?" DeeDee squealed with excitement.

Balto looked up for a second, before continuing to chew on his toy rabbit.

Dana Donnelly, showbiz and entertainment correspondent for the New Day NW morning television show, was as famous for her exploits off-camera as on. She was as well-known as most of the people she interviewed on the show, and had been photographed in compromising clinches with various A-listers on more than one occasion. No one had any idea how her husband felt about those indiscretions, since for all intents and purposes she was also happily married. Regardless of the details of Dana's private life, it was her self-deprecating humor and ability to bring out the vulnerable side of celebrities live on the air that made her such a hit with viewers and New Day NW guests alike. The year Dana stumbled and was caught by George Clooney on the red carpet at the Oscars, she got more column inches than Jennifer Lawrence, who won the Best Actress award.

"Are you listening, Balto? This is big. No, this is huge!!" DeeDee had kept New Year's Eve free, since Jake had talked about the two of them doing something together. They still hadn't finalized any plans for the night, because Roz's wedding had been the high priority for the holiday season. "I'm sure Jake would understand if I take this catering job on New Year's Eve, isn't that right, Balto? I mean, who wouldn't?" She watched Balto wrestle with his toy and sighed. "I don't know why I bother telling you anything."

She thought about calling Jake to discuss it, but there wasn't much time before she had to leave for Seattle, and anyway, she'd see him later. If she pulled off a successful party at Dana D's, it could open other doors for bookings in a much higher range price bracket. Then maybe she could cut down on the amount of work she was taking on. Surely, Jake would be happy about that.

DeeDee wrote down Dana's number. There was no time to call her before her appointment with Francesca, but if Dana really did want to hire her, she supposed that calling her later wouldn't be a problem.

She lifted Balto's leash off the hook in the hallway, and he looked up expectantly. "It's time to go get the ferry, Balto," she said, looking around for her purse. Balto spit out his toy rabbit and came bounding across the room. He leaped up on DeeDee, who was unable to clasp his leash to his collar until she'd calmed him down. "How come you ignore me until I say something you think's fun, huh?"

DeeDee had read somewhere that a dog can understand one hundred and sixty-five words, but she knew that for Balto, the word 'ferry' was probably numero uno.

The high winds on the ferry crossing from Bainbridge Island to Seattle didn't curb Balto's excitement. If anything, he was more thrilled than usual. If DeeDee had a dollar for every time he tried to jump up on the side of the passenger deck, it would have paid for lunch. As it was, by the time they arrived at the Girl and The Fig restaurant, both DeeDee and Balto were exhausted, Balto from his doggy Olympics, and DeeDee from her efforts at trying to prevent him from ending up in the Sound.

The restaurant had a dog friendly patio which is one reason DeeDee had specifically asked to meet Francesca there. Francesca looked up and waved to them. DeeDee and Balto made their way across to where she was sitting.

"Nice to see you again, Francesca," DeeDee said warmly, extending her hand. She noticed Francesca's greeting was friendlier than the first time they'd met, although not by much. At least this time, Francesca made eye contact with DeeDee.

"What are you having?" she asked Francesca, as they looked at the menu. "I'm tempted by the spiced lamb meatballs with couscous, dates, and spicy yogurt sauce. Have you eaten here before?"

Francesca shook her head. "I think I'll order fish. I'm watching my figure for my wedding."

The waiter arrived with water for them, and DeeDee ordered the meatballs. As an afterthought she added, "And the semifreddo with chocolate sauce and toasted pine nuts for dessert, please." DeeDee justified the dessert as research.

"I'll have the grilled halibut with fruit for dessert." Francesca snapped the menu shut and shoved it at the waiter. She opened a notebook and gave DeeDee a forced smile.

"So, DeeDeem what does Tink have in mind for her wedding? Didn't she think it important to come today? I'm not a mind reader, you know."

"Um, Tink had to work," DeeDee said. "Of course she'll be very involved with everything, but she wanted me to try and secure your services as soon as possible. The wedding is coming up and it's all rather sudden."

"I see," Francesca said, raising an eyebrow. "It's like that, is it?"

DeeDee didn't bother correcting her. She was disliking Francesca more with each passing minute.

"It's planned for Easter time," DeeDee said. "Apart from the dress and the reception, I have no idea what else needs to be done before then. Roz said that there were so many things you just took care of that she hadn't even thought about. We decided it would be best to get you involved from the very beginning."

"Indeed," Francesca said. "That's usually the best approach. Let's start with the venue. Does she want a church wedding, a civil ceremony, or does she have somewhere else in mind? You have no idea of the weird locations some people want for their wedding. One couple recently wanted to take their vows on the Pacific Northwest Bridge and then bungee jump off of it."

"Wow! I think Tink would want to be married in a church," DeeDee said optimistically. She'd never discussed Tink's wedding preferences with her, as her daughter didn't have a serious boyfriend, but DeeDee hoped when she was ready to get married, it would be in a church.

By the time they'd discussed Francesca's recommendations for caterers, wedding stationery, florists, bridal limousines, bridal gowns, and wedding favors, their entrees had been cleared and they were waiting for dessert.

"I guess we need to talk about your fee," DeeDee said. "Can you give me an estimate of what the total amount is likely to be?"

Francesca shrugged. "It depends what decisions are made about the arrangements. Obviously, the more I'm personally involved, the higher the cost. Since you were referred by Roz, I guess I can give you a small discount. The fee for her wedding was on the high side, but we can discuss a range once you give me a better idea of what Tink wants."

"I see," DeeDee said. The waiter brought their dessert, and DeeDee waited until he had left before continuing. She observed Francesca closely as she spoke. "You really did a beautiful job on Roz's wedding, so we're very interested in hiring you. Of course, it's such a tragedy that Clark's uncle was murdered. That's caused a lot of distress for everyone."

Francesca shifted uneasily in her seat. "It certainly has. The final account for The Catch restaurant still has to be settled, so I imagine they're not too happy. I'm probably out of pocket for the remainder of my fee, and now Clark won't get his inheritance, because he'll be going to prison. That pretty much sucks all round, I'd say."

"Excuse me?" DeeDee was taken aback by Francesca's response. Seeing her companion's reaction, Francesca started to backtrack.

"I mean, of course it's terrible for poor Roz. I do feel sorry for her, because her life is pretty much over. I guess she'll be spending her weekends visiting Clark in prison. It's just too bad, but you never know about people, do you? Sometimes it's the ones you least expect."

DeeDee pressed her. "Do you really think Clark did it? I mean, I've had doubts about him myself, but I never wanted to say anything to Roz. I'm kicking myself now, because it's too late. Maybe I could have saved her a lot of heartbreak if only I'd spoken up sooner."

"That's too bad," Francesca said. "Of course, I couldn't say if it was Clark or not. I never would have thought of him as a murderer. Maybe it was somebody else, but I was in and out of all of the rooms, making sure everything was going as scheduled. I certainly didn't have time to notice if someone wasn't at their seat. They could have been in the bathroom or outside smoking."

"Hmm, of course," DeeDee said, still closely watching Francesca. The woman was avoiding making eye contact, and she started stuffing her notebook and phone in a large canvas tote. Either DeeDee's gaze was making Francesca uncomfortable, or something else was.

"Actually, I have another appointment. Here's some money for my half of the check," Francesca said, throwing some bills on the table. She got up abruptly, startling Balto who was dozing at DeeDee's feet. "Please call if you'd like me to meet with you and your daughter, or if you have any questions."

As Francesca turned to leave, a sheen of perspiration on her upper lip was clearly visible, even though it was quite cool on the patio.

"I think she knows more than she's saying," DeeDee whispered to Balto, who was sniffing around for any crumbs that might have been dropped. She looked down at the money on the table. "A measly ten dollars? I'll be interested to see what the others make of this when I tell them about it."

CHAPTER EIGHTEEN

By the time DeeDee arrived at the Starbucks in Pioneer Square, the others had already arrived. She'd spent a little time after lunch shopping for holiday gifts, and had picked up a few things for Mitch and Tink that they'd been dropping hints about. Her children were very adult in all other areas of their lives, but when it came to birthdays and the holidays, they reverted back to their childlike selves.

She'd been hoping to buy something for Jake as well, but had come away with nothing. The minefield of present buying for a boyfriend of six months was a dilemma that was new to her at the ripe old age of forty-nine-and-three-quarters. She didn't want to spend too much or too little, especially since Jake had just told her that he loved her. On that front, she was kicking herself for not telling him that the feeling was mutual.

Jake's eyes lit up when he saw DeeDee, and she headed for the empty chair beside him. The others were gathered around two wooden tables they'd pushed together. Starbucks was buzzing with people on the holiday countdown, and festive Christmas music was playing. If it weren't for the somber faces of their assembled group, they could have been mistaken for a bunch of friends just meeting to catch up on the news of what was happening in their lives.

Al was dressed from head to toe in black, accessorized with his signature sunglasses. Roz wore no makeup and looked pale and

116

drawn, and the usually immaculately dressed Clark was unkempt and clearly hadn't shaved. Despite his poker face, DeeDee could tell that Jake was tired and worried. Dressed for the cold December weather, DeeDee peeled off her coat, hat, and scarf before sitting down next to Jake and savoring the warmth of the steaming cappuccino he silently handed her.

"I talked to Sean Meade," Jake said, " and he told me he left the wedding early." Turning to Clark, he went on, "Sean admitted he had some issues with your promotion at work, and he was guilty of having bad feelings about you before your wedding. He said he's going through a divorce right now, so your happiness wasn't making him feel very good."

Clark nodded, and made no comment.

"Sean's been seeing a neighbor of his when he's home, a woman named Monica," Jake continued. "Monica was there when I visited him, and she confirmed Sean was with her from around 9:30 p.m. Saturday on. That was too early for him to have killed Vinny."

"Yeah," Al agreed. "I was with Vinny until 11:30 p.m. Looks like Sean couldn't have done it."

"Yep," Jake said. "I also spoke with Ted Brownsdale by telephone this morning. He said Sean was one of the best employees he had, and the whole thing had been a huge misunderstanding. Apparently, Sean is next in line for a promotion, but he didn't receive the message. Ted said he felt really sorry it had caused problems for Sean."

"I'm glad it wasn't Sean," Clark said flatly. "We used to be good friends. I feel bad for not having been more sensitive to his personal situation. Hopefully, we can get our friendship back on track. If I'm not in prison, that is."

"You ain't goin' in the slammer," Al said in a gruff voice. "So quit that loser kinda talk, will ya'?"

Jake coughed, commanding the attention of the group again. "The thing is," he said, "I talked to my contact at the Seattle Police Department. Sorry to say this, but he did confirm that the police are trying to build a case against Clark, based on the fact that he was the heir, and so many people had heard Vinny say that."

"See?" Clark said. "I'm going down for something I didn't do. Roz, I'll understand if you want to divorce me. I can't expect you to waste your best years standing by a convict." He buried his head in his hands, and DeeDee saw that he was trembling.

"Shh," Roz said, her eyes glistening. She put her hand on his back, and Clark straightened up. "You're not going anywhere, and neither am I. So just listen until we're done, okay?"

Jake looked at Al. "My contact told me there were rumors over the years that Vinny had been involved in some illegal things, but they never could find anything. He said he knew one of the members of the force, John Denton, had been doing some work on it, but so far he hadn't gotten anywhere. That's the cop you were looking into, right?"

Al nodded. "Yeah. Denton's been snoopin' around tryin' to get dirt on Vinny for a while. Thing is, I went to Denton's house. His neighbor told me John's wife had a baby girl Saturday night, and John was with her at the hospital. No way he coulda done it."

Roz frowned at DeeDee.

"Somethin' else," Al said. "Vinny's lawyer, Dom Langello, made Vinny put a contingency clause in his will. If Clark ever gets convicted of any felony, he won't inherit a dime, it all goes to Cecil Larkin instead. I also got to talkin' with a woman who knows Cecil's wife Theresa. She tol' me Theresa'd been tellin' her 'bout the weddin'. When I spoke to the guy Theresa was sittin' next to at the reception, he goes and tells me Theresa had a gun in her purse."

There was a long pause in the conversation while everyone digested that information. DeeDee gave Roz what she hoped was a reassuring smile.

"Jake, did yer' guy at the Police Department mention what kind of a gun was used?" Al asked him.

"It was a large caliber gun, not a .22, so Theresa's gun couldn't have killed Vinny," Jake confirmed. "DeeDee, how did you get along with Francesca earlier?"

All eyes were on DeeDee. "I think," DeeDee began, "that Francesca's hiding something. She was very unsympathetic about Clark's situation. Roz, I hate to tell you this, but she seemed to be gloating about everything that's happened and how it could negatively affect your life. When I tried to press her on it, she got up and left in a hurry. I know it's sunny today in Seattle for a change, but it's still cold out there. We were sitting outside on the patio, but Francesca's face was wet with perspiration."

It was Clark's turn to reach across to comfort Roz. "What do you think we should do?" he said.

Jake spoke up. "Rob and I can look into Francesca in the morning and see what we can find out. Does that sound okay with you, Al?"

Al nodded. "Sure." He raised his sunglasses and looked at each of them in turn. "Ima have to go. Gotta coupla appointments. Be seein' ya."

Balto looked up as Al was leaving, and DeeDee watched him pad along behind Al to the door. The big man crouched down and spoke to Balto, ruffling his fur, before Balto turned and came back to their group. Al left without a backward glance, pulling his phone out of his coat pocket as he strode out the door.

*****

Back at Clark's condominium, DeeDee and Roz were clearing up after dinner, while Jake and Balto sat with Clark. Jake was trying his best to be upbeat, but Clark's mood was draining. Balto was being playful, and the dog was a welcome diversion from the elephant in the room.

"What kind of a dog are you thinking of getting?" Jake asked, giving Balto his rabbit toy and commanding him to sit.

Clark leaned in to Jake. "I wasn't that crazy about the idea at first, but now I'm thinking maybe it's not such a bad idea. You know...in case Roz is by herself. I'd like to be sure she's safe if I'm not around for a while. A long while."

Jake regarded Clark. "I know you're worried, but you have to stay positive for Roz's sake, if not your own. Even if the worst were to happen, and you get charged, that's not saying you'd ever be convicted. You were with John when Vinny left the restaurant, and you didn't go outside after that until you were leaving with Roz, right?"

Clark hesitated for some time and then said in a halting voice, "There's something I haven't told you. After a couple of minutes, I followed Uncle Vinny outside, but I couldn't find him, so I came back inside."

"You're just telling me this now? Your whereabouts until the time of Vinny's death will be confirmed through witnesses and hopefully, camera footage, although I'm hoping the camera didn't pick you up going outside. Even so, my guess is, should this case go to trial, it will get thrown out of court."

"I didn't think it was important," Clark said but Jake held his hand to stop Clark from speaking further. Jake glanced at his phone which had started to buzz. Jake hurried out of the room into the hallway, making sure to pull the door closed behind him.

"Don't say nothin'—jes' listen," Al said at the other end of the line. "I know who killed Vinny. I want ya' to go to the address I'm about to give ya'. The door'll be open. Jes' go on in. Got it?"

"Yes," Jake said. "Shoot." He'd just finished tapping the address

Al had given him onto his phone when the door from the kitchen opened and DeeDee's head appeared.

"Everything alright, Jake?"

Jake smiled. "I think so, but I have to go out for a while. Tell the others not to worry, I have a feeling things are about to take a turn for the better." He lifted his coat off the rack. "It's nothing bad, I promise. Come here." Holding DeeDee close, he could feel the tension in her body. Later, when he got back, he'd make a special effort to rub the knots out of her shoulders.

"Stay safe," she whispered, kissing him as he left.

In the car, he removed the small jewelry box from his coat pocket containing the gift he'd bought at the Lisa Esztergalyos store earlier in the day, and placed it in the glove compartment. It wasn't the most expensive jeweler in Seattle, but the quaint store had exquisite and unusual pieces in the quirky style that DeeDee adored. The vintage diamond eternity ring was a one-of-a-kind piece that Jake hoped would signify his commitment to DeeDee, until they were both ready to take the next step. He didn't want to scare her off, but that hadn't stopped him from planning another surprise, for New Year's Eve, one that he hoped she would love.

Pulling up at the address Al had given him, there was no sign of either the black sedan or Al. Walking up to the front door of the nondescript house, he looked around to make sure no one was watching him and gave the door a slight push.

Sensing something was amiss, he pulled his gun from its holster and walked slowly down the short hallway in the direction of a door with a glimmer of light shining from under it, his gun leading his way. There was no sound other than his quiet tread on the worn carpet. Pushing the door open with his pistol, the sight of Francesca's body caused him to freeze. She was sitting upright in a chair at the dining table, her hands tied behind her back. Her body was lifeless, caused by the bullet hole through her heart, from which a pool of dark blood oozed onto her clothing.

Walking into the room, Jake saw a gun laying in front of her on the table. On the wall behind her were numerous framed photographs showing Francesca holding various trophies and prizes. In one of them, Francesca was proudly holding the same gun that was now laying on the table in front of her. In the photograph, she wore a gold medal around her neck and a sash that declared her "Sharpshooter of the Year."

Putting his gun back in his holster, Jake reached into his pocket and pulled on the protective gloves he always carried, before lifting the first of the two sheets of paper on the table. It was handwritten and was a short confession to the murder of Vinny Santora, evidently penned and signed by Francesca Murphy. The second piece of paper, written in spidery capitals, was addressed to him.

Jake

Francesca Murphy murdered Vinny. Have the police compare her handwriting to the writing of the confession. They'll match. She admitted to me she'd murdered Vinny and used the gun that's on the table. It'll match the gun that killed Vinny. By the time you read this I'll be gone. I'd like to know what happens. Please write me and tell me when it's over. The address where you can reach me is below as well as a telephone number if you ever need to reach me.

In the world Vinny and I grew up in, 'omerta' is a way of life. I have avenged the murder of my friend Vinny Santora.

Wishing you all the best

Al

EPILOGUE

A relaxed and suntanned Al walked out of his beachside villa in his bare feet holding the US postmarked letter in his hand. Although his daily wardrobe of black had been replaced with army green cargo shorts and a white polo shirt, his ever present sunglasses were still firmly in place. Settling onto the chaise longue, he whistled to his faithful new friend, Red, a handsome Doberman pinscher he'd bought the week before, who trotted across the deck to lie down beside him. Lighting a cigar and drawing a puff, Al looked out at the sparkling blue vista of the Caribbean, contemplating his daily grind of R & R. It had been an interesting couple of weeks. He was enjoying his villa, had a new dog and a new life, one that despite some initial reservations, he found he was beginning to enjoy.

He slit the letter open with the army knife he kept on the table next to the chaise, right beside his revolver. It may have been paradise, and he was in a gate-guarded community, but he knew if someone wanted to get to him they could. The revolver was a comforting reminder of his old way of life.

Sipping his Tortuga rum drink, he opened the letter and started to read.

Dear Al,

I hope this finds you well. I'm writing to thank you. While everything you did goes against what I believe in, I want you to know I understand why you did it.

And who knows? It's hard for me to admit, but if I had been in your position, I might have done the same.

You not only avenged the life of your friend, Vinny Santora, you also freed his nephew. The case was wrapped up with the death of Francesca Murphy. You were correct that Vinny's death was attributed to her, based on the forensic handwriting analysis and examination of the gun used. I know that you would not have stopped your quest for justice until the real killer was found, and I admire and respect your unwavering loyalty to Vinny and Clark.

After the last few days, things here are getting back to normal. Christmas is almost here, and Roz and Clark went on a belated honeymoon. They'll be back in Whistler in a few more days. Clark's project there is ending soon, and I understand from Clark that there won't be any problems with the distribution of Vinny's estate. When they return from Whistler, they'll move into the house Vinny bought for them on Queen Anne Hill.

DeeDee's catering business is doing really well. She's sorry she didn't have a chance to get to know Vinny, because she thinks she really would have liked him. On the other hand, I have to admit I think it's better they didn't have the opportunity. I confess to suspecting Vinny may have liked DeeDee a little too much.

It promises to be an interesting New Year, since I'm involved in a number of cases, and although I'm doing well with them, I'm sorry you're not around. Rob, as you know, is a master at getting information, and told me you called him for Francesca's address before going to her home. I would have enjoyed the opportunity to work with you, although I have to tell you, walking into the room and finding Francesca's body won't go down as one of the most enjoyable moments of my life. The police grilled me for a long time as to how I happened to go there and find her. I told them time and time again that I had received an anonymous telephone call telling me to do that. I think they finally gave up and decided to just wrap up Vinny's murder.

That's all for now. If you ever do come back to the United States, give me a call. I'd like to buy you a beer.

You take care,
Jake

RECIPES

BEEF STEW WITH BARLEY

Ingredients:
2 ½ pounds beef sirloin tip, cut into 1 ½" chunks
1 lb. crimini or button mushrooms, cleaned
2 cups fresh spinach, cleaned, and roughly chopped
3 cloves garlic, minced
1 tbsp. tomato paste (I've started buying packets or tubes of tomato paste, so I don't end up throwing out what's left in the can.)
1 tsp. thyme
1 tsp. oregano
¼ tsp. kosher salt
2 tbsp. olive oil, divided
1 large onion, diced
1 large carrot, diced
1 stalk celery, diced
1 ½ cups red wine (I prefer a pinot noir or cabernet sauvignon. Always use a wine that you'd enjoy drinking. The better the wine, the better the dish.)
3 cups beef stock, homemade or made from a concentrate
1 bay leaf
½ cup quick cooking barley

2 cups water
½ cup parsley, chopped

Directions:
Preheat oven to 450 degrees. Add the mushrooms, spinach, garlic, tomato paste, thyme, and oregano to a food processor and pulse lightly until the vegetables are diced and the mixture comes together.

Pat the cubed meat with a paper towel to absorb the excess moisture, so it will brown. Season beef with salt. Add one tablespoon of olive oil to a large ovenproof pot over medium high heat. Brown the beef in batches. Remove with a slotted spoon and continue to brown the rest of the beef.

Add the remaining olive oil to the pot, then add the onion, carrot, and celery. Sauté for 5 minutes. Turn the heat down to medium and add the mushroom mixture, mixing well. Place the meat back in the pan, add the wine, stock, and the bay leaf. Cover the pot and place it in the lower part of the oven. Cook for 40 minutes.

While the beef is cooking, add the barley and the water to a medium pot. Bring to a boil, lower the heat, and simmer for 10 minutes or until tender. Strain out any excess liquid.

After 40 minutes, remove the pot from the oven, discard the bay leaf, and stir the cooked barley into the stew. Return the pot to the oven for an additional hour. (I've cooked it for an additional two hours, adding a little water as needed, and it was delicious.)

Serve the stew in shallow bowls, garnish with parsley, and enjoy!

IRON SKILLET GRILLED MUSHROOMS FOR BEEF

Ingredients:
1 cup white mushrooms, quartered with stems removed
1 cup Portabella mushrooms, stems removed, and sliced into 3 or 4 pieces

4 tbsp. unsalted butter + extra, if needed
2 cloves garlic, minced
Lawry's lemon pepper to taste (If you don't have it, you can substitute salt and pepper.)
Cast iron skillet

Directions:

Place the mushrooms in a heavy cast iron skillet. Add butter, garlic, and seasoning to taste. Place the skillet on a preheated barbecue gas grill over medium high heat and cook for 6-8 minutes. Add more butter if necessary to fully coat mushrooms. Remove when browned and the mushrooms are still firm. Spoon mushrooms over steak or grilled beef.

SEMIFREDDO (PARTIALLY SEMI-FROZEN ITALIAN DESSERT) WITH CHOCOLATE SAUCE & PINE NUTS

Ingredients:
2 egg whites
1/3 cup sugar
1/3 cup water
1 ¼ cups cream, whipped
2 oz. pine nuts, lightly toasted in a pan
3 ½ oz. dark chocolate, finely chopped
¼ cup fresh cream
Plastic wrap

Directions:

Combine the sugar and the water in a saucepan and heat to make a simple syrup (That's when the sugar and water have lost their separateness and come together.) Whip the egg whites with a hand-held electric mixer until soft peaks are formed.

Pour the syrup mixture down the side of the bowl into the egg whites and continue whipping them until the bowl is cool to the touch and the mixture is fluffy and thick, somewhere between 6 and 10 minutes. Fold the whipped cream and pine nuts into the mixture.

Line a loaf pan with plastic wrap. Pour the mixture into it and freeze until firm. (3 to 4 hours.)

When about ready to serve, heat the cream in a double boiler. (You can make one by putting a bowl on top of a pan of simmering water.) When the cream is hot, stir in the chopped chocolate. Turn off heat. Stir until the chocolate has melted and the sauce is smooth. (I usually make this ahead of time and just reheat in the microwave.)

Unmold the semifreddo mixture, cut into slices and drizzle with chocolate sauce. Enjoy!

SPICY LAMB MEATBALLS

Ingredients:
1 ½ lb. ground lamb
2 tbsp. unsalted butter
1 ¼ cups onions, finely chopped
1 tbsp. finely minced garlic
1 ½ tsp. ground cumin
1 tsp. ground coriander
½ tsp. turmeric
1 jalapeno pepper, finely chopped (If you don't like things really hot, you may want to leave this out.)
1/3 cup fresh parsley, finely chopped
1 tbsp. fresh orange juice
2 tsp. fresh orange zest
1 egg, slightly beaten
½ cup fresh bread crumbs
Salt and freshly ground pepper to taste
Parchment paper

Directions:
Preheat oven to 375 degrees. Heat a large frying pan over medium high heat and add butter. When melted, add onion and cook for 2 minutes, and then add garlic and the jalapeno, if you're using it. Cook for 3 minutes. Stir in cumin, coriander, turmeric, and cook for 1

minute. Remove from heat and let mixture cool for a few minutes.

Put the lamb in a large mixing bowl and add the contents of the frying pan, bread crumbs, parsley, egg, orange juice, orange zest, and salt and pepper to taste. (If you like it salty and peppery you add more of each, that's all "to taste" means. Only you know how much you want to taste the salt and pepper.)

Mix thoroughly by hand and form into meatballs about the size of a golf ball. Place on a parchment lined baking sheet and bake in oven for about 20 minutes, or until golden brown. Remove from oven and serve with a sauce of your choice. (I like them over rice with a yogurt sauce.) Enjoy!

IT'S AN EMBARRASSMENT DESSERT!

Ingredients:
1 loaf Italian or French bread
1 jar of Nutella
Tin foil

Directions:
This is so easy that I'm embarrassed to put it in a book, but every time I serve it, people ask for the recipe, so here goes!

Preheat the oven to 300 degrees. I slice the bread in half lengthwise, and then I slice each half into thirds. (Trust me, this is really loose, so if you prefer to cut the bread into neat slices, that works as well.) Wrap the pieces in tin foil and put them in the oven for about 10 minutes. You just want to warm them.

When they're ready, take them out of the oven and smear Nutella on them or put the Nutella in a bowl and let your guests smear to their heart's content. Yep, it's that easy, and ohhhh sooo gooood! Enjoy!

Paperbacks & Ebooks for FREE

Go to www.dianneharman.com/freepaperback.html and get your FREE copies of Dianne's books and favorite recipes immediately by signing up for her newsletter.

Once you've signed up for her newsletter you're eligible to win three paperbacks. One lucky winner is picked every week. Hurry before the offer ends!

ABOUT THE AUTHOR

Dianne lives in Huntington Beach, California, with her husband, Tom, a former California State Senator, and her boxer dog, Kelly. Her passions are cooking, reading, and dogs, so whenever she has a little free time, you can either find her in the kitchen, playing with Kelly in the back yard, or curled up with the latest book she's reading.

Her award winning books include:

Cedar Bay Cozy Mystery Series
Kelly's Koffee Shop, Murder at Jade Cove, White Cloud Retreat, Marriage and Murder, Murder in the Pearl District, Murder in Calico Gold, Murder at the Cooking School, Murder in Cuba, Trouble at the Kennel, Murder on the East Coast, Trouble at the Animal Shelter, Murder & The Movie Star

Liz Lucas Cozy Mystery Series
Murder in Cottage #6, Murder & Brandy Boy, The Death Card, Murder at The Bed & Breakfast, The Blue Butterfly, Murder at the Big T Lodge, Murder in Calistoga

High Desert Cozy Mystery Series
Murder & The Monkey Band, Murder & The Secret Cave, Murdered by Country Music, Murder at the Polo Club, Murdered by Plastic Surgery

Midwest Cozy Mystery Series
Murdered by Words, Murder at the Clinic

Jack Trout Cozy Mystery Series
Murdered in Argentina

Northwest Cozy Mystery Series
Murder on Bainbridge Island, Murder in Whistler, Murder in Seattle

Coyote Series
Blue Coyote Motel, Coyote in Provence, Cornered Coyote

Midlife Journey Series
Alexis

Website: www.dianneharman.com, **Blog:** www.dianneharman.com/blog
Email: dianne@dianneharman.com

Newsletter

If you would like to be notified of her latest releases please go to www.dianneharman.com and sign up for her newsletter.

Made in the USA
San Bernardino, CA
01 August 2020

76379793R00093